BURNOUT

BURNOUT

A Novel

Tanner Peterson

ISBN 979-8-9952365-0-4 (Paperback)
ISBN 979-8-9952365-1-1 (Ebook)

First Edition: March 2026

Published by Tanner Peterson
United States of America

For anyone who burned too bright, too fast.

Prologue

As I ran towards my house with Lily, the rain hammered down, pelting my body. "I don't even think she grades correctly," she said, skipping along beside me. "It's like she has it out for us." I adjusted the strap on my backpack that never seemed to fit. "It's just a couple more months, and then we won't have to deal with her ever again. She'll be gone from our lives forever."

Lily smiled at this. "Forever? She'll probably still haunt my nightmares with her atrocious fucking grading."

I laughed and told her I agreed. It was March, and school was ending, and we didn't have to worry about the world. Our biggest problem was one bad teacher, but we'd still pass.

"When we get inside, I'll go ask my dad for some money and we can see the new movie," I said to Lily as the rain started to pick up.

"What a gentleman you are to leave me out soaking in the rain, Mikey," she said, motioning her hand at me. She was always like that, playful in a flirty manner. I smirked and told her she could stay inside, of course. We were close, and our families were too. I might have my dad come down and say hi to her. It just depended on his mood. Lately, he'd been acting strangely, and his doctor had been giving him pills hand over fist.

When I arrived at my house, I opened the door with my key and told Lily to stay downstairs. "I'm going to wash up in the bathroom," she said in a matter-of-fact tone while she scrunched up her blonde hair. I watched her for a second, then turned away only to catch her staring at me. I conceded and put my backpack down, taking a seat to think about my day.

Sitting down, I glanced out the window. Wishing I had a drink or a Coke, I tried to distract my mind. The back windows all showed the rain hitting them, enough to wake someone up. Was my dad up? I could go ask him for some money for tonight. I didn't want to be a burden, though. I hated being a burden and rarely found any company other than Lily and my parents. That was one thing I didn't want to screw up.

My mind never let me be still. It was always rushing to the next thing, the next problem, the next move, as if standing still meant everything behind me would finally catch up.

Thinking about my dad, I'd noticed irregularities in his behavior over the past few months. He seemed almost paranoid and didn't have as much money as he used to, even though he'd told me many times he had more than enough. I'd tried to ask him about it, but he'd shrug it off and say he was seeing a doctor. One time he'd said "shrink," but then claimed it was a joke. I felt bad asking, but I had no job and wanted to take Lily somewhere fun. Such a dilemma, I thought, shaking my head.

As I went upstairs, I stopped to look in the bathroom mirror. My brown hair was plastered to my forehead with water, making it look black. I needed a comb and opened the cabinet, which was littered with pills. I had no clue what any of them were, but I was sure some had to be the ones people at school sold. The kind you'd find at your grandparents' house, stockpiled to the heavens, just waiting to be abused or taken.

After finding the comb, I dried my hair and made myself look more presentable. Walking towards my room, I got to my dresser and changed clothes, trying to make myself look better for Lily. I hope I don't look like such a failure, I thought. I'd heard that word once when I was eavesdropping on my mom and dad arguing about bills.

"He could get a job and help us out if he wasn't such a failure."

I wasn't sure who said it, but deep down I knew. I wasn't a failure. I was set to graduate next year and start working in town.

It made me angry to hear this from them. If anything, my parents were the failures. My mom had started drinking when my dad would leave on drives at night, and they never spoke to me. Never a "Hi, Michael." Never a "How was your day?" Never "Are you feeling okay?" I didn't want them to do this because I'd feel embarrassed. I wished they'd put effort into it. I was their only child. Maybe even a simple damn compliment would go a long way.

I heard a knock on the door and froze. I was so in my head I'd forgotten what I was doing. "Yeah, Dad, I'll be out in a minute," I muttered. The door opened and Lily came in, which annoyed me. "We'll leave in a minute. I was just getting dressed."

She paid me no attention as she held out two bottles of pills. She started to get excited, and this annoyed me more. "What is it?" I asked, trying to contain myself.

Lily looked at me. "Do you know these are all painkillers and benzos?" I stared blankly at her. Those words were foreign to me, and I didn't understand why we were still in my room. I didn't do drugs or give a shit about them. They wouldn't affect my brain.

"Look, we have to take one right now to make our day better," she said with an urgency I hadn't seen from her before, unscrewing the cap. I was too annoyed to argue, so I took the pill she gave me. She swallowed hers and motioned for me to do the same. I swear she had me under a spell because I did everything for her without question. After I swallowed it, it tasted chalky and gross, and I wanted to spit it out but didn't want to embarrass myself in front of Lily.

"Okay, seriously, Lil, go wait downstairs so I can get us some money." She nodded gleefully, and I watched her go down the stairs. I had no clue what I'd just done. I'd stolen medication from my dad. My chest ached, and I felt terrible about it, and now asking for money would feel even worse. What if the pill actually affected me and I did something stupid, like the people on those dumb TV shows?

Knowing I'd be sober for a bit, I took the chance to walk down the hall from my room. I went to my dad's door and tried the handle, which didn't open. He never locked his door, which made this odd. "Dad?" I asked aloud. I heard nobody upstairs. Something felt wrong. I used my key, always hidden atop the door frame, and opened the door, telling him, "Okay, I'm coming in."

A terrible smell washed over me as I called out to him. I didn't want to believe my eyes as my body started to shake violently. I felt as if I were watching myself through a movie projector. Nothing made sense. I fell to my knees and threw up, staring at the ground. I tried to find the strength to get back up, but there was nothing there. The room was hell, and I was stuck without the use of my senses.

I reached over to the bedframe and used all my might to pull myself up. I fell onto the bed and found I was covered in red. Blood was all around me. I raised my hand and watched it drip onto the bed and off my fingers. With my eyes slowly focusing, I saw him. My father was sitting in front of me with his eyes rolled back into his skull, slouched over to the left.

"Dad?"

I shook his arm.

"Dad?"

I shook his other arm.

"Dad, wake up. Dad, please, look at me."

The grotesque image of what was once a human didn't move. I stared at him. I don't know why. I could see a gun next to him and a hole in his head. I wanted to look away, but I stayed there. I kept asking him to wake up.

"Dad. Dad. Dad. Do you know how good my day was today?"

I began to laugh. Hard. He didn't find it funny, as nothing moved. I couldn't stop laughing, and soon the laughing turned into a horrendous cry.

I sat there crying for however long, until I heard a scream behind me. My mind was so fucked that I didn't care to turn around. Arms were placed around me as I was dragged out of the room. I didn't move much or hear anything except for someone on the phone. I drifted in and out of consciousness and finally saw what I thought to be Lily.

"Take me outside, please," was all I could muster.

Her hands guided me through the door as I heard sirens in the distance. The rain poured down hard enough that mini lakes had started forming. I stepped outside and looked up at the sky. I saw nothing as the rain blinded me. I looked down and saw a sea of red leaving my body. The red pouring off me had turned the mini lakes blood red. In the distance, two birds ran for shelter from the rain. Perhaps they weren't running from anything, I thought. Maybe they were enjoying it. I wished I could do that, I felt, as I sat down in the rain.

I could hear Lily yelling at me to come back inside, but I didn't move. I sat there as the sirens got closer and closer. It was a strange feeling, knowing these sounds were coming directly for you, and you were embracing them. My soul felt empty. Nothing felt real. I laid myself into the water, looking at the sky. I could see red and blue lights in front of me as I lay there. The rain kept hitting me, reminding me of what had happened. Blacking out, I remember staring at the sky and seeing two birds dancing, a dance in circles, over and over again.

A Start of Ren

I sat outside my therapist's office, wading through the newspapers. I hadn't wanted to be here, but my mom had made me come since the police told her it would be a good idea. She'd been fixated on therapy ever since, and I'd begrudgingly agreed to come one time. The memories of what happened didn't stay with me most of the time. They felt distant. Whenever they appeared, I tried to block them out. It was like running away from the memory and never wanting to relive it. Now here I was, alone, waiting for my therapist, the memory replaying in my head over and over.

My mom hadn't come. Her health had declined significantly, and she opted to stay in bed most days. Days after it happened, her doctor had started giving her pills, which she took in the morning and during the day. I rarely saw her anymore as she confined herself to her room. In my own house, I felt completely alone and miserable. In her drugged-out tone, she'd come over to me while I was eating and told me the therapist in town would be seeing me.

"It's expensive, Mikey. You have to go for your health." I'd said whatever and agreed to go. As I sat in the chair, I felt a mix of emotions. Anger mostly, but love deep down. Maybe this would fix me, I'd secretly hoped.

The therapist came out. "Hi, Michael. My name is Dr. Angela. You can come in now." She looked normal enough, and I nodded as I walked in. I'd been nodding to people a lot more lately, since I didn't like to talk as much. I'd become an introverted recluse, and when people spoke, I felt uncontrollable anger that they could live their lives without worrying about what people like me had gone through.

She walked me in, and I stared blankly at the window behind her chair, where I could see the parking lot. Angela sat down in front of my view, which snapped me back. I took the chair next to the door. Good for a quick escape if I needed one. She turned to her desk, grabbed a clipboard, and turned back to me. "So, Michael, why do you think you're in here today?"

I didn't want to be hostile, so I responded with an unintentional bitterness. "My mother wanted me to go to therapy. And here I am." She nodded and stayed silent, waiting for me to say more. I felt annoyed, but I had an hour to kill, so I figured I might as well get it over with. Talking to someone other than Lily might help for a change.

"My father killed himself, and I saw what was left of him, and uh, I don't know, my life just really seems to suck? I don't know what seventeen-year-old should be going through this, you know?" I said, trying to get things out of my mind and into reality.

Angela scribbled down notes, then looked towards me. She adjusted in her chair and spoke. "What you've been through, nobody should ever have to go through. I'm here to help you work on anything that's bothering you."

I gave her a dry "Thanks" and returned to staring at the window while some birds flew by.

"Have you noticed any changes in your personality since it happened?" she asked.

I ran my hand through my hair. "I feel more anxious. I can't sleep as well, and I get angrier than I used to. Not in a physical way. It's more like in my head. I can imagine myself flipping out when something happens that I don't like."

Angela kept taking notes, which made me feel like this was a job interview from hell where she was collecting all my secrets. She looked up from her notepad. "What you're experiencing is normal after such a traumatic event. I'll be able to have a psychiatrist prescribe you something to help. It's completely optional."

I replied with a nod and felt anxious as I watched her scribble more. She ripped a piece from her notepad and handed it to me. It had her name and two phone numbers. "The first one is my work number, and the second is my personal number if you ever need counseling immediately," she said as I took the piece of paper.

"Thank you," was all I could muster.

"I don't think we need to dive deeper into the subject today. We can talk next week. And if you pick up what I'm sending to the psychiatrist, it could help too. The local pharmacy in town." She turned away, stood up, and walked towards the door.

I got up and walked out, thinking I wanted to say more but didn't know what. It was an itch in my brain that I couldn't scratch. How could I say something like "I want to stop running from the things I see in my mind and be at peace" without sounding like a psycho? I thought about next week and remembered she'd said something about the pharmacy, which was on the way home. Why not stop and pick up whatever medication they'd give me? I could probably sell it at school to buy some soda for the week. I started on my way.

A walk through my town consisted of the same buildings everywhere, the same weather, the same people. It was like a never-ending existence of replications, and it wasn't that I hated it. I quite liked it. It made me feel at home. Passing my school, where I'd be starting my senior year in a couple of days, I couldn't help but sigh. Dealing with school on top of everything else would be annoying as it was, and I was already waiting for it to be over before it started.

The only good thing would be seeing Lily again. My only friend. What a failure I was. At least she made school bearable. I had plenty of people who didn't like me for fuck knows why. Maybe it had to do with teachers giving me special treatment after my father died. Or maybe the guys who hit on Lily were jealous of how close we were. That thought was too far-fetched, and I knew it.

Coming up to the pharmacy, I walked to the window and rang the little bell. The lady stared at me emotionlessly until I said, "Do you have anything for Michael Ren?"

She walked away and came back with two bottles of medication, told me to follow the instructions on the labels, and handed them over. "Don't I need to pay for this?" I asked. She looked at me oddly and finally spoke. "It's already been paid for."

She walked away from the window, leaving me holding my medication. I didn't understand and assumed it was a mistake on their end. I brushed it off, knowing it would have only been a couple of bucks anyway. Not that I wasn't grateful. I barely had any money, and neither did my mother.

Walking home, I read the pill bottles in my hand. One read Prozac, to be taken daily. The other read Alprazolam, to be taken as needed. I'd heard of Prozac because my father had mentioned taking antidepressants before he passed. I wondered why they'd give me one, since I wasn't depressed. I decided I'd take it daily to see if it helped me regain some kind of emotional balance. The other bottle interested me more. Lily had mentioned this name before, or I'd heard it at school, and I was sure it was a drug worth something. If she'd talked about it, then it was worth taking for my mental stability.

I reached my house and let myself in with my key. Silence greeted me as I walked in and locked the door behind me. I shouted "Mom," then her actual name, "Elizabeth," a couple of times, but got no answer. I walked upstairs to her room, where the door was cracked. Taking a peek, I could see she was fast asleep. No surprise. I sighed and walked down the hall to my room. I could be alone with my thoughts for the day without her pestering me about how therapy went.

I put the pills on my nightstand, unscrewed the Prozac, and took one. Then I went to my drawers and grabbed my journal. I plopped down on the floor with my back against the bed and decided what to write. I'd always liked writing in my journal, but lately I'd open it up and stare blankly. Today felt different. I couldn't describe it, but there was a desire to write. Using the pen attached to the side, I wrote out whatever thoughts came.

Today I met with a therapist and got medication. Not too excited to take pills, but things could be better soon with school starting because I'll get to see Lily again. I stared out the window during my meeting and saw a pair of birds. I wish I could be one and fly away, to have the freedom to go anywhere I want.

I shut my journal and placed it next to my nightstand. Then I walked around the room and decided to lie in bed and stare out the window. My mind felt blank as a canvas, and my brain didn't have the tools to paint a picture of what I was seeing. Maybe I was depressed and not willing to accept it. All I knew was I had to get through this school year and go on with my life. All I knew was that I'd been dealt a shit hand and had to keep moving forward. If I lay here forever, maybe I wouldn't have to go through more pain. I closed my eyes and let my mind wander to a billion scenarios before the dark overtook me.

School Begins

Today was September 3rd, and my alarm had just gone off. My dreams evaporated, and my warm blankets would have to go. Rubbing my eyes, I sat up in bed to get my bearings. The blank walls made me feel as if I were still dreaming, and I could hear the pouring rain outside. I'd been dreading this day. Not because school was starting, but because of the painful memories of last year. I hit the alarm and saw it was 6:45 a.m. I took my Prozac and looked at the other bottle, then decided to put it in my backpack. I could ask Lily about it later.

Getting up, I got dressed. The usual sweatshirt and black pants. I looked in the mirror and saw I was wearing all black. The usual look for me. Leaving my room, I saw my mom was still asleep and the house was dead silent. Being an only child, I'd learned to deal with the quiet. I walked down the hallway on the second floor and knocked on my mom's door. She needed to be up to take me to school, or else I'd have to walk in this rain. When she didn't answer, I let myself in and saw she was passed out with her alcohol and pill bottles next to the bed. I wanted to hit the wall. You're supposed to be my mother, I said to myself. Everything had changed last year. Before all that, she was a vibrant and loving woman. Now she was barely awake when I saw her.

Knowing I wouldn't be getting a ride, I flipped my phone open and texted Lily. She'd know what I was asking. I went to the bathroom to shower, as I did every day before school. My father had always taught me the importance of routines. Without routines, humans were subject to madness, he'd tell me. If a shower kept madness away, I was okay with that. I got in, washed my hair, and hopped out. Looking in the mirror, I saw how skinny I'd become. My ribcage showed, and my thin brown hair fell to my eyelashes. I was relatively tall at five foot ten, which made people look at me strange when they saw the tall skinny kid. I didn't mind it. I didn't feel anything related to emotions of late.

While I got dressed, my ringtone went off. Lily had said yes. She'd pick me up at 7:20, texted with a smiley face. She was a blessing in my accursed life. I think I'd fallen in love with her over the past year, and I was sure she knew. But this was Lily, and I could never jeopardize our friendship by telling her.

Heading downstairs, I opened the fridge and the cabinets. Bare and empty. No food at all. I checked the table for some leftovers and saw my mom had left a note: Enjoy your first day, Mikey. She'd written it and left me two dollars. I think I knew the year was 2007, but my mom must have thought it was the sixties. Still, I couldn't complain about the state of our finances. I packed a few binders and my notebook, all blue, and grabbed my backpack.

Making sure I had my key, I opened the door, locked it, and waited on the porch. I had a couple of minutes to kill, so I flipped open my phone and stared at the lock screen. A picture of my father, mother, and me on my first day of high school. Almost the same time last year, before it all went wrong. I stared at it, thinking, Go back and revert this. Please, God. I hate how I am now.

I drifted off into my thoughts and was met with a memory. I had tried to suppress them all lately, but this one stood out. I think all this talk of my dad had made me realize how much I missed him.

In my head I could still picture it because it was so fresh. The warm night air. The lights of the stadium. I was in the dugout being called up to bat for Ashford High's baseball team.

As I walked up, I remember looking around to see Lily, who gave me an energetic wave, and my dad watching with his face pressed against the gate.

"You got this, Michael!" he told me with a smile.

I waved him off and shook my head with a smile. It was so embarrassing of him to do, but I was glad he was here. At least he cared enough to see me strike out, which I always did.

When I got up to the plate, I knew the pitcher would smoke me. But I got into my stance like my dad had practiced with me and aimed for the stars. I wanted to make him proud. To hit it once.

The ball flew right by me. I didn't swing. Strike one.

Lock the fuck in, I told myself. I watched the pitcher. I knew he wouldn't throw the same ball twice. That was a fastball. This would be a changeup, no doubt. I waited on it.

I stood there as I watched it soar into the sky against the backdrop of stars. I heard my dad yelling "Run!" to me, but I just stared at it.

It felt like it would stay up there forever, and by the time I moved, the outfielder had caught it.

I walked back to the dugout and saw my dad at the gate and passed by him. "I didn't think I'd actually make contact."

My dad laughed. "Sometimes you just need to try. You always tell me you can do anything. So why not hit a baseball?"

I smiled and walked back to the dugout, where I sat next to my teammates.

Thomas slugged me in the shoulder. "You're supposed to run when you hit the ball. I know you're not used to that."

I shrugged. "Does it really matter if I got on base, Thomas? I hit it to the sky."

Thomas replied, "And you watched it fall. Into the outfielder's mitt."

All I did was stare out at the field. "What goes up must come down."

I just wanted to be that happy kid in the picture again. But I'd concluded long ago, as many humans throughout history have, that you cannot change the past. My phone flashed "Here," and I saw Katrina pull up to the driveway. If last year was the worst year of my life, maybe fate had a twisted sense of humor and would make this one better. I walked out, got in the car, and sat next to Lily, wishing fate would intervene. Just this once, I asked in my head.

· · ·

Katrina told me how happy she was to see me and asked how I was doing. "Same old, same old," I replied in a melancholy tone. She said how glad she was that I'd called Lily for a ride. Katrina had become a kind of mother figure in my life ever since last year, and I appreciated it. I didn't know how to express this. It had just happened naturally, since my own mother had basically given up. I told her I enjoyed the gesture and would pay her back, to which she replied, "Just watch over Lily here," with a wink towards me. Lily stuck out her tongue and glared.

She pulled out her class schedule, and to my surprise we shared most of our classes. A wave of happiness washed over me for one split second as I pictured us sitting together. I hated interacting with strangers, and teachers loved pairing up random students. Going to Ashford High was a strange sort of experience. Most of the teachers didn't care about the students, which wasn't entirely their fault, as the students had no intention of learning. If you wanted to learn something, or be around people who wanted to "broaden their horizons," as one of my teachers would say, you had to take the honors courses. For me, that meant all honors: English, Math, Chemistry. The rest of my classes didn't offer it.

Lily was in honors with me, too, which started last year. I believe that's how we became close, since in a regular class I'd have had no reason to talk to her. She was outspoken and bright when she wanted something done, and I liked that about her. When we'd partner up, I'd do most of the work and let her handle the presentations because she understood I hated public speaking. She could see when I was uncomfortable and was always ready to step in. We'd passed our honors classes last year because of this. In general, the classes were a nice fit at my weird high school.

Unfortunately, ever since last year, I hadn't been doing well in my studies. Many of my teachers gave me a pass because they knew what I was going through, but that grace period runs out. You can only say "I'm the depressed kid who went through trauma, please excuse my poor performance" so many times. The sadder thing was I didn't believe in myself to do better this year. I was becoming like the other half of my school. The people who had no care for education and did whatever they wanted just to get by.

I knew most of them, having gone to middle school together, and I'd never been particularly popular. I was what you'd call the silent loner. People knew me, and I had some friends, but they weren't friends I could count on outside of school. For example, one of them, Thomas, was the spitting image of the other kids at Ashford High. They'd do drugs, skip class, party, the rest. In my recent state of mind, I envied them. I wished I could forget everything and drown my brain in substances. Deep down, though, a part of me wanted to succeed in life, or at least high school. But that was very deep down, and I felt like I could succumb to that life on any given bad day.

Katrina arrived at the parking lot, snapping me back to reality. She told us good luck, and Lily and I hopped out. Lily looked at me, smiling. "Ready for our best year yet?" I told her the bar was very low, and she grimaced. Walking inside, we went down the long corridors to the only class I would come to care about: Honors English.

I walked with her behind me to the back of the class, in the corner, which I'd recently started doing. I figured the teachers would leave me alone, and for the most part, they did. I hoped that wouldn't change. "Back of the class is where it's at, apparently," Lily said, looking at me. The tables filled up, and before I knew it, our teacher walked in.

"Welcome to Honors English 2, where we will learn much more than just regular English grammar." A few groans.

"As I'm sure most of you know, I'm Mr. Wright, and I want to get to know all of you this year. I hope it isn't too early to jump into our first assignment?"

Great. Eight in the morning and I already had to write. I didn't mind writing. I just thought I'd have a couple days of freedom. Mr. Wright spoke again. "You are to write on half a piece of paper what you did this summer, and what you want to achieve by the end of the school year. Five minutes."

Could I write lying in bed and wanting to die? Could I add that I hoped a car accident would hit me by the end of the year? I'd done nothing this summer except wallow in depression, and I had nothing I wanted to achieve. I wrote down: This summer I did nothing, and what I hope to achieve is being able to do something. I thought that sounded smart, at least. I'd see what others said and maybe change my answer.

The five minutes were up. Mr. Wright stood. "Okay, we'll start in the back there. Young man, would you care to introduce yourself?" It took me a moment to realize he was talking to me. I pointed at myself in question, and he nodded. I had horrible anxiety and could feel my heart hurt, but I forced myself up.

"I'm Michael Ren, and I don't enjoy many things, which is why this summer I didn't do much of anything. If I'm being honest, I don't like many things or humans for whatever reason lately. What I want to achieve in this class is being able to do something, if that makes any sense."

I sat down and waited to hear what he'd say about my rather pathetic description. I hadn't meant to say I didn't like humans. I'd sounded like such a moron.

"Well, Mr. Ren, it seems like you're in a bad place, or being a bit of a misanthropist, if you don't mind me saying so. You always need a goal in life, something to work towards. I want to help you with that this year. Thank you for sharing." I'd never heard a teacher talk to me like that. He gave me a dry smile. I had no clue what "misanthropist" meant, but I had no time to think it over, as Lily stood up right next to me. The teacher didn't even need to call on her.

"Hi, I'm Lily, and this summer I was able to work with my mother and go see parts of nature around the state. For this class, I want to get to know everyone and get an A." A classic response from her. She wasn't afraid to say anything, I thought as I looked at her standing next to me. I wished I could be more like her.

"That's an excellent goal, and I'm sure you'll get there with that attitude, Lily," Mr. Wright said. She sat down, pleased with herself, and smiled at me.

This went on until the end of class, when the teacher told us there wouldn't be any homework for the next month. Everyone was happy until he said he wanted us to keep journals and update them daily. He wouldn't be reading them. It was just for us. I thought this was odd for an honors class, but I didn't mind.

The rest of the day was uneventful. My teachers went over rules and explained how the tests would work. I zoned out through everything, thinking about Lily, whom I'd seen earlier with another group of students. We were supposed to walk home, which made me irritated that she was with other people, but it would be unfair to control her life. I tried not to think about anything and looked out at the sky. The rain had stopped, but the clouds still loomed. I loved the clouds and the rain, but not at school. During the summer, I'd stared out my window at them for hours, watching them move, watching the rare glimpse of lightning. Since these weren't honors classes, Lily wasn't in them, and I had no one to talk to. My brain and my thoughts were my only friends. Behind me, I heard people talking about which drugs they had and were going to try after school. I wished I could have said, Take my Prozac, it'll cure all your problems. I thought that would have been funny. Other than that, I had straight contempt for everyone around me. Nobody knows what I'm going through, I thought. These thoughts ended as the bell rang.

Getting out of class, I knew Lily would be at the front entrance, and my last class, science, was the farthest from the front of the school. With anxiety racking my brain, I stopped at the bathroom to take one of the pills that read "take as needed." But when I walked in, I saw my friend Thomas and his friend Connor. Thomas did a double take at seeing me and gave me a weird look, which confused me. Connor came over, and I felt myself shoved against the cold wall.

"What are you doing?" I asked, confused out of my mind. I didn't know Connor all that well, but Thomas should have stopped him.

"Stay out of our business or you're going to find out what happens, Mikey, and it isn't fun," he said, letting go of me with a shove. Still confused and shaken, I looked at Thomas, who was calm, then back at Connor.

"I don't understand what the hell you're talking about, Connor," I said to his face. Thomas stepped forward as it was clear Connor was about to throw me again, or worse, and just shook his head.

"Just don't get in the way. This isn't for you," he said, and he and Connor left the bathroom. I tried to understand what the fuck had just happened. I stretched my right hand and tried to feel something but didn't find anger. Just hate for humans like him. I opened my backpack and took my pill, still trying to figure out what business I'd supposedly interfered with. This was probably some drug bullshit, and I'd been in the wrong place at the wrong time. I flexed my right hand again, making sure I was alive. Next time someone laid their hands on me, this hand would make them bleed.

Clouds and Other Dark Things

I met Lily near the front entrance. I'd texted her I would be there, but she'd beat me to it. I realized I was starving when my stomach started to grumble. With the money situation going on, I'd become accustomed to one meal a day, or just a snack, and it was taking a toll on me. Maybe that's why I felt so weak with Connor earlier. I needed to be prepared for next time.

Since it was a small town, there wasn't much to eat at except Tracy's Diner, which happened to be Lily's favorite place. She'd known the owner for years and would always go there when she was in a good mood. I knew she'd want to go today, but I didn't want to tell her I was dead broke.

She stared off into the distance until I got right to her. "Took you long enough. We should go to Tracy's. I need a Coke after today." We both loved Coke, and I think one of the worst parts of being poor was being unable to afford something as simple as a drink you enjoy. Not wanting to ruin her mood, I told her we could go and started our walk. The diner was situated towards the center of town, five minutes from both our houses and fifteen minutes from the school, which made it a hotspot for all the kids in the area.

Walking there was like listening to a happy dog bark at you after not seeing you all day. "All my other classes were fun, and the people in them didn't seem to care about it, which means it'll be an easy class," Lily said as she told me everything about her day.

I think she told me she was taking creative writing or something in the fine arts, but my thoughts had drifted to the incident earlier, and I was left staring up at the blank sky. This morning it had been raining, and now the sky seemed dark and gloomy. I could only describe it as if the sky had been angry before and now had become sullen.

"And you?" I heard her say. Looking ahead, I told her the people in my class were like hers and recounted the incident with Thomas and Connor. Then I told her about the pill I'd taken and its name, as I'd started to feel weird. My story came out jumbled, and I wasn't sure if I'd gotten the message across. Simply put, that was all I could remember.

She looked at the ground, only a minute or so from the diner now. "I wish I could try them sometime. They always seemed so off-limits that I almost want to see what they do." She seemed to skip over the story with Thomas, which I found odd, but my mind was drifting. I'd never heard her express this about drugs, but honestly, I felt the same. If there were a magical pill that could make all your pain go away and your days turn into nothing, I would be on it constantly.

I looked again at the sky, and now, instead of sullen, it seemed flat-out depressed. "For two," she said as she walked in. The waiter who seated us seemed familiar, but I couldn't place his name. I suppose he'd gone to our school at some point. Lily didn't need a menu, as all she ever got was a Coke, fries, and a sandwich. I'd always thought this was funny because who eats fries with a sandwich? I guess that's what made me like her so much. Being different. Being eccentric. Being beautiful. The complete opposite of every girl in this town. Grabbing the money in my pocket and not wanting to take it out, I looked at the menu and saw that a fountain drink was $1.89. Perfect, but imperfect. I guess I wouldn't be eating today.

The waiter came, and when it was my turn, I ordered a fountain drink. Both of them kept looking at me as if I was going to get something else, so I had to say, "That's all." When he left, Lily looked at me funny. "Not to be your mother, but you're going to starve yourself. I'll share with you."

I told her it was fine and gave her other excuses, but when the food came, she gave me some fries and a piece of her sandwich, which at that moment I was eternally grateful for. I rummaged around for my money and put it on the table. I believe she realized that was all I had on me and understood.

"You could have just said something. My mom will always give you extra money." That was the problem, though. I didn't want to freeload off anyone, even if my situation was dire. There were enough problems on my plate, and I didn't want to create more for others. I thanked her and told her it was fine. I'd have more next week.

After paying, we left and made our way to her house, as going to mine would have been an utter embarrassment, which I believe she knew. Staring off ahead towards our neighborhood, she looked at me funny. "I think we can solve your money problem."

I doubted anyone could do that, but I didn't interrupt. "It's not all for you, though. I want to earn money too. I've seen people, or at least heard of how you can make some pretty easily." The last word of her sentence reminded me of what my dad had always told me: nothing in life is easy. It also popped into my mind, very randomly, that Thomas could be connected to this.

"The thing I told you about what happened after school in the bathroom. Does this have something to do with it?"

I asked her as the rain started to fall. Lily looked over with an odd smile. "Kinda, but I'll tell you all about it when we're at my house. Promise." I nodded and looked at the sky while holding my hand out to see if it would catch a falling raindrop. I asked what this brilliant plan was.

"I didn't say it was brilliant, but I can show you in a couple of minutes if you're a little more patient," she said with a wink. With that, we were at her house. Before I walked in, I turned around to see the clouds. It had started to pour.

Plans

Katrina wasn't home, as she worked until seven o'clock most days, so we had the whole place to ourselves. I didn't know much about Lily's father, just that he'd passed when she was very young. I suppose maybe that's why we got along so well. I'd heard of mutual trauma and the bond it builds. Maybe in another life both our fathers were alive and we never met. It didn't matter.

Walking up the stairs, we headed to her room. Her upstairs floor plan consisted of her parents' bedroom, a bathroom, and the hallway that led to her room. I always liked how minimal it was. The room she had was always beautiful to me. The curtains were shades of dark blue, and the walls were set up to match them. Her bed sat in the corner where the front reached the window, so you could see everything happening outside while lying down. She had a nice navy blue rug that I'd seen more times than I could remember, and a mini couch to go along with it. For such a small room, it felt spacious and cozy.

I went over to the couch and sat down. Lily dropped her backpack and was changing her sweater, which was soaked through. I realized mine was too, so I took it off and put it on the ground. The warm air in the room was a nice contrast to the day outside. I kept thinking about what she'd said about this plan of hers, so I asked her straightforwardly. Not looking at me, staring instead towards the hallway, she told me, "We earn some easy money if we work with Thomas and sell the pills he has."

She stopped and waited for an answer. I did not expect this in the slightest, but I had nothing to lose, and the notion that Lily wanted to sell drugs was funny to me. Even if it failed, it would be a fun experience, I assumed. Looking at her, I replied, "So this is why Thomas and Connor were mad at me? Do you want to undercut them, or am I missing something?"

To this, she looked bewildered. "I talked with Thomas about doing it, but I never mentioned anything to Connor."

Looking at the ground, I thought for a moment. "It doesn't matter anyway. But why do you want to do this?"

Lily smiled at me in a way that made me melt. "I want to feel something in my life for once. If you want to do it and it makes us some money, I don't see the harm in it. Everyone at our school already does it. We aren't sinning or doing something evil."

I nodded. "You're not worried about getting in trouble with the law or your mom?"

Lily motioned out towards me and shrugged. "I could ask you the same thing."

I wanted to laugh. My mom was the biggest drug addict now, and if I got in trouble with the law, I was sure she wouldn't care or would even be awake to know I was gone. Curtly, I told her, "To answer the question, no, I'm not worried in the least."

She looked pleased and told me she'd already talked to Thomas about getting them. He was willing to give her a hundred pills for free the first time if she was able to pay him sixty percent of what they made. I thought that might be decent money, but I had no clue how much a pill was worth, so I asked. Pointing her hands and using her fingers to tell the story, she replied, "Well, technically the street price is five a pop, but I figured we could overcharge for six or seven to people who need them at parties or whatever."

Her reasoning was solid, and I told her, "Why not." She got up and gave me a hug, which was very unexpected for a drug-dealing discussion. I loved feeling her skin on mine. "Thank you so much, Michael," she kept saying, but I didn't hear any words. I just felt her close to me. I wanted to tell her how much I cared for her and how I would never let harm come to her.

"He gave me five for free, so I figured we could each take half of one," she said, getting close to me and making my mind wander. I'd never taken any drug before, so I asked her simply what it does. "Takes away your anxiety. Makes you sleepy. Makes you tell the truth."

I had no clue what "tell the truth" meant, but I told myself I could figure that out later tonight. I figured now was the time to mention the medication I'd gotten. Digging into my backpack, I grabbed the bottle and tossed it to her. "Is this the drug you're talking about?"

I already knew the answer before the bottle hit her hands. She did a double take. "Yes, but this is an actual prescription. Here, we can try it together right now," she said, splitting one in half and handing me a piece. I told her I'd already taken one today, to which she promptly said, "Double the fun." Not wanting to let her down, I asked if she had any water. I always had to take pills with water, or my OCD would get the best of me. I hated the feeling of pills stuck in the back of my throat. She got up and said she'd be back with some.

I watched her walk down the hall and looked at the pill. It was a tiny rectangle, all white, with the word Xanax on it. I felt it wouldn't affect me since I'd already taken one today and had never done drugs in general. I just thought my brain would automatically block whatever the pill was trying to do. I'd never thought I could get high unless it was one of the drugs from the movies, the ones you saw homeless people using. The ones you shot into your arm that made you slump over. Those people were dead as they stood there. I'd seen them in the city. They're like me, I thought. Just dead on the outside, not the inside.

Lily returned and tossed me a water. Putting herself back down against the bed, she looked over. "Bottoms up." I told her it wasn't a drink, but I understood. It couldn't hurt to see what it did, and besides, if I did want to help her sell it, I needed to know what it would do. I took the pill and swallowed it with the water in one gulp. I looked over at Lily and told her quite frankly that it wouldn't affect me, to which she just laughed and said, "Tell me that again tomorrow, Mikey."

I wondered how long it took to kick in. I learned that it doesn't respect anyone but natural law.

Suddenly, I realized I was lying in her lap. Lily was awake, looking at the hallway, and I was just there. I didn't understand. It felt like a dream. So I dreamt. The next thing I knew, we were walking down the street holding hands. What a strange dream this was. I never dreamt. When I did, it usually ended with seeing my father alive or dying, depending on how my day had been. My dreams were just dreams I couldn't use to escape from reality. It was a game of Russian roulette: would I see my father's blood-soaked corpse or dream about a girl I loved?

Now we were grabbing Cokes from a diner, and Lily was talking to me, but I didn't understand what she was saying. She kept telling me how cute I looked, and that she was going to have to watch me all night. I realized I was leaning against a wall. I could barely stand. My dream switched again, and we were with some boy from my school whom I recognized but couldn't place. I overheard him say something about me. My brain didn't want to hear it. I saw them exchanging a bag. We were walking away now. We were going to my house.

"You told me nobody would be home, right?" How did anyone know that? Was it Lily? I tried to say yes, but just a nod came through. When did I tell her that? How did I know that? Was I lying?

Now we were in my house. My room. My non-decorated room. I couldn't see out the window. I rolled over and saw Lily talking to me. "I just took one so I can sleep. Tomorrow we need to go to school."

I had no clue what she took. Or for that matter, what she meant. My hair was being played with. I felt her hands run through it. I was facing the window and I couldn't see her. Was it Lily? I didn't know. I wanted to sleep forever. This ongoing dream seemed to be the best place to be.

My world, filled with the things that I only wanted. Lily next to me, not thinking about the past or school, running around town. I had no pain, no suffering. Everything was a bliss of love and light. I felt her grab me tight, and then all I knew was endless darkness, as if the evil in the world had destroyed my perfect sweet thoughts.

Sweet Dreams

I don't remember when I came to. I didn't know what had happened. Had anything happened? I opened my eyes but didn't move. I could see light, but I didn't know what my body had gone through. My memories were not my own, as if an alternate reality had mixed with mine and taken over. I didn't feel afraid. I didn't feel anxiety. I felt nothing. Nothing in the best way possible. As if I were a human who didn't have to suffer.

Suddenly, I became aware of something attached to me. I looked at my stomach and saw hands. This should have scared me, but again, I felt nothing. An overlapping theme of what I would feel, I'd started to think. I held them and turned around to see Lily in my bed, holding onto me. She looked so pure, lying down like an angel. I didn't want to disturb her sleep.

It occurred to me that I should check if she was alive. I don't know why I thought this. I think it was because she looked like she wasn't even breathing. I felt her heart and was reassured. I moved her hands over to hold them in the middle of the bed. Whatever reality I was in, I reached out to God. Make it last, I asked. Fate can be cruel enough. I needed this more than anything.

Being shaken, I saw Lily talking to me, but I didn't understand her. I mumbled out a hi, and she finally stopped. She let out a sigh of relief and went back to sitting on the bed. Finding my voice, I asked, "Where am I?"

She looked at me like I was crazy and curtly replied, "You're in your bed. At your house. Where else would you be?" I knew this, but I didn't understand what had happened. My brain felt as if things had happened and not happened. Explain to me, I said. I want to know, I reiterated, placing my hand on her shoulder, which she pulled away from. I didn't understand why she would do that. She'd had her arms around me before. Finally, I felt emotion. Sadness washed over me all at once. I couldn't control it. "Lily, what happened to me? My memories feel mixed, and I don't know what to do. Are you angry at me?" I put out every word I could think of. Something was wrong.

"I learned a lot about you last night. You acted like a real human for once," she said, playing with her hair.

"I also think you're in love with me. But I don't mind that." She paused. "You took a pill yesterday, but it was too much for you. You'd never taken anything before and your body couldn't handle it. I met with Thomas to ask him about it. He said the ones he gave me were stronger than what most people start on. I got a new bag of 2mg off him. I know I don't have the money, but he said not to worry about it and he'd get what he wanted." She said all of this in quite a disturbing manner, which I didn't understand.

"We need to pay him back. We need to sell the drugs and give him his share, or I'm fucked." My head still burned, but I knew I could fix it. I could fix anything if I wanted to, especially for her. The things we do for love, I thought. I told her to let me get my head in order and we'd get it fixed. The way she looked at me made no sense. She'd said she knew I loved her. Did I know what love even was? I'd lost all my emotions over time.

"I know you're confused, Mikey, but today we meet with one of his customers. We need to sell the initial pills and the new ones. I saved ten each for both of us, because fuck all the trouble we had to go through. And for God's sake, I thought he killed you."

I thought he'd put me in a much better world. As I lay there thinking about what she'd said, her talking about customers had confused me. She got her water and took a half pill. "We have to go meet in an hour, at the water tower. I need you to do the talking. I don't want to even think about what Thomas told me."

I still felt out of it, but hazily agreed. The urge to ask for another pill was high, but I needed all my brain power because who knew what a "customer" even was. I was certainly meant for these situations, but not when I felt like I was in La La Land. I had a chance to prove myself to her. I got up and immediately regretted it. I asked her to get me some Advil from the bathroom, and she recommended I take half a Xanax for my head.

I thought this over and decided the pain needed to go. My talking and plan might not be as good, but I dealt with enough damn pain. She tossed me a half and went to get the Advil. I didn't know what to feel except looming despair. When she walked back in, she handed me the Advil, which I graciously gulped down and prayed to God it would make me feel better. I knew we'd have to get moving since the water tower was to the west, opposite the school at the edge of town. I looked at her and told her I was ready to go, and I would lead.

We didn't say much as we walked. I caught a few occasional glances from her that I didn't know how to read. She looked as if she were hiding something, or guilty. Not wanting to pry, I kept walking. My head had calmed down, and I felt a little woozy from the half pill. I practiced words in my head and made sure I didn't slur any of them. I hadn't done anything on this scale in my life. Why would Thomas have us meet a customer if he was selling directly? It made no sense to my brain, but I told myself to keep walking.

When we arrived, the sky was a dark blue and the forest had grown all around us. Like most of the parts of this town, it was abandoned and left to rot, now a landmark and a gathering spot for illegal activities. How did I get myself into this, I wondered. I rested against the ladder at the tower and told Lily I would do my best.

That's when I heard footsteps and hoped Thomas had come to greet us. I could deal with Thomas on the fly. If it was someone else, though, I didn't want to think about that. To my dismay, it was not him. This man looked to be about six feet tall and had an ugly stare. The type of person you'd pass on the street and get a shiver down your spine seconds later. I noticed the tattoos on his arm and wondered if he'd been to jail. But my thinking was cut short.

"Are you the ones selling?" he said in a disgruntled voice. It sounded like he was more annoyed than angry. I didn't know if he'd mistaken us or if this was a terrible coincidence, but for some reason my brain responded. "Yes, we have what you want. I'm guessing Thomas sent you?" This was the best reasoning I could think of. No way some random person would show up at a designated time. Still, I wondered why Lily had even agreed to this with Thomas. Maybe she hadn't.

He looked me up and down, sizing me up. "Let's get this over with. The hundred 2mg for seven hundred, like I was told." I didn't have them on me, but Lily finally seemed to come alive and handed the bag to me. I knew I couldn't just give him the drugs without the money, so I asked, "And you have the seven hundred ready?"

He pulled out a wad of twenties. I didn't want to stand around counting them, so I took the chance that Thomas hadn't sent a moron to scam us. We met in the middle, and I handed over the pack first. He opened it, bit down on half of one, and spit it out.

"Yep, that's alp alright. Here, kid." He passed me the bills, which I put in my jacket pocket. "And a word of advice. Next time you're out here selling, you should ask who I am. Cops hang around these parts."

For such a scary man, I thought this interaction was strange, but I thanked him. I watched him walk away to the left, and soon he was gone. Looking behind me, I saw Lily, who hadn't spoken once. Something was wrong with her.

"Lily, we need to go now. I don't want to be here any longer." As I said this, she looked at me with dead eyes. Almost emotionless.

"Please take me back to your house." I looked at her again and could see her starting to cry, shutting down. I grabbed her hand and walked her away from the water tower.

The whole way home, not a word was said. This should have been her moment. She'd set all this up, and we had seven hundred dollars on us. Yet nothing was said. Her hand felt cold in mine, and I felt cold in my body. With my other hand, I flipped open my phone to call my mom to see if she'd be home. It rang and rang until it went to voicemail, which, annoyingly, was full. She was probably passed out or somewhere doing God knows what. Can't even rely on my goddamn mother anymore, I said to myself as I rolled my eyes.

Getting into the house, I brought her to my bedroom. I helped her get most of her clothes off and put all my blankets on her. I was going to ask what I could do for her when she spoke aloud to no one in particular.

"Thomas told me if I kept this up and wasn't able to provide, he would. He would hurt me. I've wanted to throw up ever since he told me this. I took two pills and yet I feel nothing. I need you, Mikey. I'm scared. I should never have done this. Please, deal with him. Then we'll move on."

I was astounded that Thomas had told her this. The happiest girl I knew, and he'd told her he would hurt her, which I could only guess by her reaction meant something beyond my comprehension. I sat on the bed and looked at her. "Lily, I'll fix this. Stay in bed for the rest of the day and rest."

She let out a sniffle and told me I was undeserving. "I will protect you, even if I'm the scrawniest kid, a dumb kid. I will do anything to keep you safe. You mean so much to me that I couldn't even tell you."

She kept staring at the wall, then looked up at the window. "But, Michael, you have told me. You have."

Confrontations

To say I was pissed was an understatement. I'd never been in a fight before. I'd gotten my ass kicked in middle school and my nose almost broken, but I'd never thrown a punch. All I knew was Thomas had to pay. Before I left, I made sure Lily was tucked in and grabbed my dad's old bayonet in case things went south. The thing was supposedly used in the Korean War, and my dad had gotten it at a garage sale. "I completely fleeced the guy!" I remembered him saying. It was sharp, but I needed an actual plan. Lately, I'd been going into situations without thinking, which wasn't like me. Talk to him. Ask him about our share of the money. And get him to fuck off about Lily.

That seemed like three good points I could focus my conversation on. I opened my phone and hit call on his number. When he picked up, all I said was, "Meet me in front of the school near the parking lot in twenty minutes." I hung up after that. I didn't want to hear his fucking voice more than necessary.

Lily was stronger than I was in every aspect of life. She looked after me. Her mom cared for me when mine didn't. This was much too far. What kind of fucked-up kid says shit like that, I thought. I knew dealing drugs was bad, but threatening her? Even if it was a sick joke, he needed to pay.

Arriving at the parking lot, I checked my watch. The lume in the dial was shown by all the lights I'd passed. 7:37. I'd called him fifteen minutes ago and decided to wait. I felt around in my pockets and realized I had the other half of the pill I hadn't taken. Having no water, I dry-swallowed it. Instantly I regretted it, as it tasted like chalk and made me want to vomit. I made a mental note to always take them with water from now on.

Reminiscent of the strange man earlier who'd bitten into half of one. I guess that was the way to make sure it was real. I kept trying to get the taste out of my mouth by swallowing and questioned why I'd taken it in the first place. I was nervous, but I didn't need it. It wouldn't happen again. I sat there waiting until 7:45, when he finally showed up. He looked drunk or high and just plain stupid. "Mikeyyy," he said, giving me a crooked smile.

I wanted to turn that smile into pain. Think clearly, I told myself. "I sold your drugs. You didn't show up."

His smile went away when he saw the look on my face. "That was one of my customers. James. I don't like to sell to him."

"So you wanted Lily to sell seven hundred dollars' worth of drugs to a guy that you don't even like, which God forbid makes me think that man is dangerous. Not to mention what you said to her."

I could hear the snarl in his voice as he responded. "She came to me asking to sell drugs. I told her if she couldn't provide money, then we'd compensate in another way."

Not wanting to hear this moron talk about her like that, I countered. "Speak like that again and I will kill you." I felt the bayonet against my skin itching to be pulled out.

He walked up right to my face, and I awaited the inevitable punch. "You aren't a tough guy, Michael. You're not made out for this, and you're not a killer, and your bitch isn't either. I've known you since you were a kid. You're broken. Nothing can fix you. Selling drugs won't fix what you're running from."

My heart jammed hearing this. I pulled out the bayonet and twirled it up and down. I had no intention of using it, but that level of disrespect warranted showing it. "We'll be keeping the seven hundred. We'll sell the rest of the 2mg, and then we're done. But you got one thing wrong. If you hurt Lily or talk to her like that again, you won't see me coming. It'll just be all black for you."

Next thing I knew, he'd dived on top of me. The knife was knocked from my hand under the van next to us. I crawled back and got up while he held onto my ankle. With my left foot free, I bashed it into his skull. Instantly, I felt his grip release. I dropped to all fours to find the knife and was reaching for it when my head was kicked in.

You never know what actual pain feels like until your head has been kicked into concrete. My vision wobbled. "You're done for. I could finish you off right now. You think you're the only one who has nothing to lose? Grow up. Why do you think I do this?"

He ranted on about his life, but I focused on the knife. So close, and my vision so blurry. I grasped the hilt and held my arm still under the car so he couldn't see I'd gotten it. "You shouldn't have called me out here tonight. You don't want to give me my sixty percent?" He laughed hysterically.

Pure evil radiated throughout this kid, I thought. This wasn't just his doing. Connor must have turned him into this. "Lily will pay for more than sixty. I can assure you of that, Mike." He went down to pick me up, and now was my chance. I slid my hand out from under the car and thrust at his side, the blade going right into his abdomen. He was still picking me up and hadn't realized what happened.

Suddenly, he dropped me. He looked around, confused. Then he saw the pool of blood on his shirt. I didn't know what to do. I'd just stabbed someone. Did I call the police? No. That would only lead to us both going to jail, and I didn't feel like that. Somewhere in my mind, his words hit me again. So I hit him. The first time I'd ever hit someone. I struck him in the jaw, and he fell to the ground. My promise had been kept. Next time, I would fight back. I stood there for a good thirty seconds trying to think of something to say to him. I just felt agony and stayed quiet.

I knew I had to go. I checked to make sure I had the knife, which I tucked in the back of my jeans. Lifting up my hands was like looking at a bloodbath. I had blood all over me. If a cop saw me, it was over. I don't want to go to jail, I don't want to go to jail. I kept repeating it in my head. I started to run towards home, but I had to stop. My skull ached. I couldn't move or think. It was piercing pain that wouldn't stop.

Fuck. I'd just committed a crime. I checked through a mental list. No cameras. No one around. No, the phone. I had to get his phone. My body shuddered, and I threw up in the bush next to me. I limped back towards where it happened. It was like how a serial killer would revisit the scene. There was blood on him, but he looked to be alive.

I couldn't think about his well-being, though. I needed the phone. My DNA was already on him, so it didn't matter if I touched his arms. I dug through his pockets: some pills, a phone, and some money. I can make this better. I put the money in his hand, took the phone, and scattered the pills along the ground to make it look like they spilled. Lily, God bless her soul, had given me some earlier, and I took mine and added those. The police would think it was a drug deal gone wrong. They had to. I wasn't going to jail for the likes of this moron.

I left and started my way back. When I was out of range of the school, I threw the phone as hard as I could at the ground. It hurt so bad to throw, and I cursed myself. Then I stepped on it. Every single time, my whole body winced. Every step was agony, but it had to be done. The phone was shattered in half. I just had to find a storm drain and chuck it down there and I was good. I kept going forward, hiding behind bushes, walking forward, just thinking that I would be able to lie down.

I finally saw my salvation up ahead. A storm drain where I could chuck the only remnant of poor Thomas's life into. What had I done? I kept asking myself. I almost collapsed with pain as my brain thought of him lying there, drowning in pain, with nobody to help him. I hadn't even connected the knife to him, but it had done something. I limped over to the storm drain and threw it down.

Goodbye, Thomas.

Now my only mission was centered on one thing. I found myself dragging myself home. Every time I saw a glimpse of headlights, I ran towards a bush or any gate that kept me out of sight. My body hurt so bad I stopped to hurl. It didn't want to cooperate with me.

I was so close to home, but my body felt galaxies away. Keep pushing, I heard my dad say. I was going crazy, hearing the voices of people who weren't there.

One foot in front of the other. One at a time. I moved onward.

I kept pushing. Only forward. Finally, I could see my street and made a last-ditch attempt. I had a frightening thought about getting caught at the last moment and made a mad dash for my house. Thankfully, I got there. I'd left the door unlocked. Stepping inside, I was met with pure silence.

The walk up the stairs hurt my head so fucking bad I nearly hurled again. I made it to the hallway and went into the bathroom to properly throw up. I grabbed three Advil and took them all. I wanted to sleep. To go to my world again. I left the bathroom, stumbling to my room. I saw Lily on the bed, fast asleep. I took a pillow from my couch and lay on the floor. My eyes slowly drifted to the window, where I thought about what had happened. If only I could stay in this moment forever and not face the consequences of my actions. The last thing I remember is looking out the window at the brightest star in the sky, with Lily right below it. Two beautiful stars right in front of me, yet both so far away.

Rude Awakenings

A combination of light and darkness filled my head, leading me to believe I was passing to the other side. I strained to open my eyes, as it hurt to move any inch of my body. I saw Lily gaping in horror at me, shaking my arm. "Mikey?" she kept whispering. Over five times she said it, as if she were unsure whether I was alive. I was annoyed by this and asked her what was wrong. The last thing I wanted to do was talk.

"Mikey, why are you covered in blood?" The questions she was asking didn't sound like her. They were one-dimensional. It was as if she already knew the answer. Her voice was soft-spoken and quivering. To the best of my knowledge, I had no clue what she was talking about. I looked at her. "What do you mean, blood?"

She picked up my arm and shoved it to where my eyes could see. My arm was a bloody mess. I looked over the rest of my body and saw the same thing everywhere. Surely if this were mine, I'd be dead, I thought. "I'm fine," I told her. I was not fine. My head felt like someone had taken a shotgun to it and I was still alive.

"Fine? Mikey, what the fuck happened to you? Your eyes can't look at me straight, and you're covered in blood, and you passed out in the middle of the bedroom with blood all around you, and you say you're fine?"

She was practically yelling at me. I asked her where my mom was, which pissed her off even more. "I locked the door before letting her in, in case you want to tell me whatever the fuck happened to you. Accidentally fight a grizzly bear?"

I tried to laugh, but nothing came out, so I just shrugged. My memories were all jumbled, and I did my best to remember, but my head. My fucking head. It hurt so bad. I asked her to get me Advil for it, and she said that could come after I told her. This was very annoying, as I felt like dying, but I suppose this did look bad on my part. I felt around my body for bruises. My thighs were fine. My hands were bruised. Then I felt my back. The knife was still held in place there. Instantly, everything came back to me. The flood of memories hit my damaged head so hard I wanted to cry.

"Lily, I will tell you everything, but for my sake, please get me a damn Advil." Seeing how much pain I was in, she passed me the pills, which were on the floor next to me, and gave me water. I took three of them. I just needed this headache to go away.

"Do you need to see a doctor?" she said with pleading eyes. That would have been very nice if I hadn't stabbed someone.

"If you're not going to answer, I think I have some idea of what happened." She pulled out my phone.

"You met with Thomas, right?"

I couldn't lie to her, and what would even be the point? I had to figure out how to get out of this once my head was back to normal. I sighed and told her, "Yes. I met up with him."

"And what exactly went on between you two?"

I flicked up my fingers. "He insulted you, so I made him pay." It made me excited to say this. I couldn't tell if I was going mad.

I even went on. "I asked him what he said to you, and he said he'd do worse."

I wanted to be the hero she relied on, so I thought, why not make myself sound better. "And I worked it out with him."

Standing over me, Lily threw an Advil at me. "The fucking blood, Mikey?" Oh yeah. How was I supposed to say I'd accidentally stabbed some moron because he slammed my head into the ground? I looked at my right arm and then at her.

"We got into a big fight over it. I think he got it worse than I did. That's why I have blood on me."

What a pathetic lie. If my head didn't feel like the Hindenburg, perhaps I could have come up with a better answer. Pacing around, she asked, "And why is Thomas not answering his phone? It goes straight to voicemail."

Yeah, straight to hell was more like it. "I doubt he wants to talk to us after the fight I got into with him."

My head didn't hurt as much. I needed to get rid of these clothes. "Lily, can you get these off me and let me shower?"

She looked at me with suspicion but agreed. I motioned towards my blood-soaked pants. "Also, just keep the clothes in here. I'll wash them myself."

Nodding, she came over and got them off me down to my boxers, and then I went to shower. The whole time, I held onto the railing for dear life. I had bruises and blood on me, but the more I scrubbed, the worse it got. The warm water hit my skin, making me want to sit down in the bathtub and never get out. I gently started to cry into the water. I thought about my dad and what I'd done with my life. My tears mixed with the blood and fell down into the drain.

How quickly life can change. Getting out, I took a look at myself in the mirror and opened the door. I asked Lily, who was sitting in front of it, for an oversized shirt. She went to my closet and got me one, which felt like heaven. In the room, I got the bloody clothes together and put them in a pile in the corner. I'd figure out what to do with those later. Her voice was soft and caught me off guard. "Michael, where is Thomas?"

She was afraid, and it was written all over her face. "I don't know, but we can go to school and see him today. What's the time?" She told me it was nine and we weren't going. But hell, I needed to be there.

Showing up late would look bad, but not going would be worse. "Listen, we need to go." My head throbbed and my vision blurred. My fucking head. She looked at me like I was crazy. "Trust me. Let's just go. It's just five hours and I can't miss today."

Lily, who was packing her things, looked up at me. "You come here covered in blood, pass out, you can barely speak, and you want to go to school? I'm starting to believe you hit your head or something."

Something sure had, Lily. Something had. She came up to me and whispered like a child. "I didn't want anyone to get hurt. I don't want someone to hurt me. It was childish of me to think selling drugs was a good idea."

My head was still spinning, but I reassured her. "Nobody will hurt you if I'm here, and it is a good idea. Accidents just happen in deals, from what I've seen in movies. It's all just a misunderstanding."

She wasn't happy with this answer. "You're downplaying it and you know it. I'm walking alone." I wanted to scream at her that I needed to be with her right now, but I didn't have the strength to argue and watched her go down the stairs. As I heard her leave the house, I punched the wall and screamed. Nobody is coming to help you. I had my head against the wall with my hands on each side. Nobody is coming to help you. I yelled at the voice to shut up and got my backpack. This is what I get for trying to help.

Leaving the house, all I felt was pain and anger. It was insanely stupid how much pain I was in and how I couldn't take it out on anything. Nobody was there to console me. I had to keep my cool, yet I felt like I could murder someone if they looked at me the wrong way. I just kept walking and told my brain to shut up and walk forward.

It hurt like a bitch to make it there, but I had to be present. If I could make it through English, I could sleep in my classes the rest of the day. They didn't matter to me. None of this did. I wished Lily had walked with me. I wished my mother had been up and seen me off to school. I felt so much hatred for myself and the world. I didn't want to do this, yet my actions had caused it, and here I was. Five hours of miserable, fucking pain just to show up.

Arriving at school, I was met with a highly unfamiliar sight. My nerves became shot, and I was unstable. I felt my brain start to tremble, my vision blur. This was real, not a nightmare. Police tape was everywhere, and news trucks surrounded the school. This can't be happening. I didn't cause this. Go away.

Why would all this be happening? Did Thomas die? It didn't matter. I had to find out what it meant. Looking over my surroundings, I saw Lily and met her eyes. She became distant, looking back at me, then towards the school. For once, I wasn't focused on her. I went forward to find out what was happening, fearing the worst.

As I got closer, I heard girls whispering next to me. "I heard he was a dealer. Maybe that's why."

He was going to be a rapist, I wanted to scream at them. I heard so many voices around me that all sounded alien. Every student was talking about it. I heard voices that were crying, and I heard voices saying what a tragedy it was. I didn't care. Move forward. I had to see what the news was covering.

Reaching the reporter, I could hear them talking. They could have been rehearsing for TV or broadcasting, but it didn't matter. What they said did. "For the first time in sixty-five years, a person has been stabbed in this town."

Sixty-five years, huh? All it took was sixty-five years for a scumbag like Thomas to come along? "We cannot release the name, but the police are looking into it as a random act of violence."

Let them.

I felt rage. Impotent rage and anger. Who cared if that worthless piece of garbage was hurt? My father died, and no news outlet ever covered his death. What was so important about this boy? He had nothing to offer the world. He only had cruel intentions and horrid goals. I started to shake with anger and felt an adult put a hand on my shoulder. "It's going to be okay," they said.

You have no clue what you're talking about, I wanted to scream. But I nodded and made my way to leave. I went through various students who looked shaken up and kept whispering about serial killers and other nonsense. I couldn't stay here, and I doubted class would even be going on.

I had a couple of dollars and some pills on me and needed to get a Coke. I started towards the diner when a hand grabbed my arm. I flinched, only to see Lily looking at me. I'll never forget that moment. No words were spoken. Only eye contact was made, and the words passed through our eyes. I felt like I hated myself, her looking at me like that. I didn't want this. I never wanted this. I kept walking and didn't look back.

Crime and Punishment

I finally arrived at the store and got a Coke. $1.67. I dished out two dollars and left, leaving the change on the counter and heading towards the water tower. I needed to be alone. As I walked, I popped two pills from my pocket. I didn't want to feel anything. I wanted to feel like I was in a dream world again. The world, the police, everything that I thought was hurting my head, and Lily. Oh, poor Lily, looking at me like that.

I was halfway there when I realized I needed her. The realization also came that the pills had kicked in. I retraced my steps and ran into her. She'd been following me. I went up to her and looked her in the eyes. "Please hold me. I need you to know more than you can imagine."

The glare on her face was one of anger and agony. "You hurt someone. You, Michael, hurt someone. You lied to me. You want me to hold you? Are you a baby in need of care?"

"Lily, you don't understand. I need you right now. Please. I can explain it all. You're all I have. Please." I was begging her. I wanted her to hug me as she had before.

"Why did you show no remorse?" she responded with a stare that pierced my soul.

"Because, well, I did it to protect you." It was the truth. From my standpoint, at least.

"I didn't ask you to hurt someone." She stopped for a second and almost balked. "Tell me why I shouldn't go to the police right now and tell them what happened." I was appalled. Why couldn't she understand what I'd done for her? I didn't want to hurt anyone. I'd tried to keep her safe. I was astounded. "I was dealing with a drug dealer, and you expected things to go smoothly? He'll be fine."

She turned sideways. "I won't tell them for now, but this was a bad idea. This whole selling drugs thing. It was way over our heads. It's probably best if we take a break from seeing each other to not attract any suspicion."

I didn't understand. "What do you mean? Lily, what the fuck does that mean?"

Lily turned her back and started to walk off. "I got in over my head and made a mistake, and it hurt you, Thomas, and me. I need time to process it, Michael."

And with that, I watched the only person I loved in my life leave me. I watched her walk and get farther and farther away. I had a glimmer of hope she would turn around and talk to me. I needed help. I couldn't do anything in my state. Lily never turned around. In a moment, my eyes could not see her, and with that, my star had disappeared, and my life was as dark as the night sky.

Do It Yourself

The next few weeks were agonizing as I attended school and watched Lily ignore me as if I were a pest. Everything I'd gone through had happened so fast that I'd begun taking my as-needed pills whenever possible. I didn't dislike Lily's idea of selling drugs, and it was the only excitement I'd had in a long time. I would figure out how to do it without her or Thomas. I didn't need anyone. Lily would get over this silliness and talk to me soon when I was making money.

Planning and thinking were all I did these days. I'd tried to get as much information on Thomas as I could and learned he was recovering in the hospital. Since I hadn't been arrested, I assumed he hadn't told the police what happened because of mutually assured destruction. This led me to think about what would happen when he got out, and to make matters worse, his lackey, Connor, had been watching me lately. He was the serious kind of creep. Not many things freaked me out, but there was something wrong with him.

I'd thought about visiting Thomas in the hospital for a brief moment. To tell him I was sorry. We'd known each other for a long time, and I hadn't meant for any of this to happen. Feeling remorseful, my mind wanted to do this, to tell him the mistake I'd made, but I was in too deep. I doubted he'd believe me anyway, so I kept to myself for the most part.

As I'd go to class and doze off on my pills, I knew I'd need a refill soon. I hoped the pharmacist would refill it and I wouldn't have to see my therapist, but that would be an issue for a different time. Right now I had to figure out how to stay low, learn how to sell drugs, and also get them for personal use. My anxiety had been sky-high recently, which hadn't helped in any way, which led me to take more of my pills. I'd stopped taking the Prozac, as I felt the Xanax took care of my issues instantly and I didn't need to be taking multiple drugs.

I was sitting in the back of the room during my last period of the day, trying not to take another Xanax, when I heard the name Thomas pop up. Could this be who I thought it was?

The kids in front of me were talking so loud. "They say he has a nasty scar on him now, but they can't find who did it. It's like some Zodiac Killer thing, but he survived it. I tried to ask Thomas about it, but he just got angry at me and had the nurse kick me out."

Thomas hadn't snitched on me? Did he want me dead? My mind swirled with thoughts. Fuck.

The other kid continued. "Yeah, I tried to talk to him too, but the cops kept going in and out and I never got the chance. They'll find out soon, though. This town is too small." He laughed. "Dumbass, you think the Zodiac would have left him alive to tell the tale?"

The other kid slugged him in the shoulder. "You're the dumbass. The Zodiac did do that." They started fighting each other, and I left the classroom and flew down to the restroom.

I threw up in a stall and tried to calm my nerves. Police? How was Thomas alive? Who would have made the call? There was too much blood.

Now was the time for the Xanax. I scrambled in my pockets for my wallet, took a couple, and walked out to wash my hands and mouth.

I stared at myself in the terrible school mirror. My face looked distorted, like it wasn't a real reflection of me. I splashed water on my face and tried to look again, but the distortion was too much.

If Thomas was alive and talking, it was only a matter of time. Someone would question me.

As I sat in class trying to get my mind off Lily, my thoughts wandered to an experience from two days ago. A girl named Nicole, whom I'd never taken notice of, had come up to me and introduced herself. I didn't know what to think of this, but I'd gotten her number, and she'd texted me, to which I still hadn't replied. Last night I'd been reading an article about misanthropy and flicking Xanax into my mouth out of boredom, only for my phone to say one new message. The blue glimmer of flicking it open and seeing Hey Michael glaring up at me made me feel strange. Everything I touched, everyone I met, turned out miserable. I didn't like people, and the last thing I needed was another liability. I'd think about it later tonight.

Getting out of school, I started my trek home with only one goal in mind. Success. Nothing could stop me when I had a goal and nothing to lose. I wouldn't let my mind call me a failure as it routinely did. I would make money and be able to show Lily that I was a good person, that I'd only wanted to help her. The whole situation was unfair, as I was protecting her, but life isn't fair. The people who play by the rules and are always earnest always lose. Suckers were the people who stayed complacent their whole lives and never questioned anything. They were made to be broken. Only the ones who had the drive to succeed could get away with it.

Getting to my house, I unlocked the front door and headed to the kitchen for food. My eyes caught something next to the kitchen that stood out like a sore thumb. The table was covered with bills. All in red lettering. I realized the house was going to be foreclosed. I couldn't be homeless at eighteen and leave my mother to rot in some shelter. I had a Hail Mary idea in that moment.

I rushed over to the water tower. I'd decided I would wait all day until people showed up and ask if they'd seen a tall man with tattoos come around this part of town recently. If he was meeting here, there was a good chance people would know him since this was the poor side of town. I walked and walked, trying to find anyone on the trail to the south side, but I had no luck. I sat down near a stream and laid my head back to face the sky and decided to wait. Going home would bring me nothing but suffering.

After a couple of hours, two middle-aged men walked near me. As politely as possible, I asked about the man. One of them laughed and said, "Trey doesn't sell to kids," but the other took pity on me and told me he shows up here around the evening. I thanked them and thought about this after they'd left. If Trey was the man I'd met before, then I could try my plan. I doubted there would be others who looked like him around here. With renewed self-confidence, I knew I was close.

I walked back to the tower and waited, alone with nothing but my thoughts. I saw Lily walking away over a thousand times. Thomas's body was covered with blood. Over and over, I sat there while my mind imprisoned me in a cell of my own doing until I heard him.

"Thomas's boy. What a weird day for you to be here."

A man had come and brought a buddy along with him. I needed to convince him to let me sell to him, but I had a slight problem with acquiring drugs.

"I've heard you've been asking about me," the man I knew as Trey said.

I stood up. "I didn't know where else to go and wanted to talk to you about it since Thomas is out of the business."

He gave me a quizzical look. "Wasn't he your friend?"

I chose my words carefully. "Just a business partner. It's unfortunate what happened to him, but I can't change the past."

He gave me a devilish grin. "Well, you aren't one to mince words, so tell me why you're here."

Here we go.

"I still want to be your supplier. I assume you sell to other people at higher prices, which is why Thomas had me sell to you. I can continue to provide that if you tell me where Thomas was getting it from."

Trey's friend erupted with laughter. His friend had such a strange look to him in multiple ways. He looked almost ghoulish, and the scary part was that I could have sworn I'd seen him before. He took out a cigarette and lit it.

"Kid, what good could you do for us?"

I told them I was seventeen years old and prepared to take any risk to make money. His friend, who he introduced as Tony, looked me up and down.

"Sure, kid, I'll help you out. He was buying them online. I can't help you with that since I'm an old man, but if you manage to figure it out, we can do business."

He stomped on his cigarette. The internet? I didn't even have a computer. I looked at him. "I'll be back here in two weeks. Then we can do business."

Tony watched our conversation closely without saying a word.

"The name's Trey, by the way, kid. Too bad we couldn't have a proper introduction. Good luck."

Before I could reply, Tony butted in. "Do you know who might have done this to Thomas?"

He knew. I shook my head.

I started to walk away. "Two weeks. I'll be back with more Xanax than you can imagine."

Walking away, I heard Trey laugh. I assessed that Trey was competent and someone I would not want to cross, and Tony was someone I couldn't get a read on. Something uncanny about him crossed my mind while walking back, but that comes with selling drugs, I suppose. I considered today a success. Now all I needed was to acquire the drugs.

Since Thomas had bought what I could only assume was a hundred, which he'd given us, I needed to one-up him to make a good impression. If I could find a way to buy around two hundred pills, I could start up a real money-making business and not have to deal with selling individually to people. Thinking all this made me want Lily at my side so we could discuss everything and plan it out. For now, I had bigger problems, though.

I needed internet access. The library would be a terrible idea. All I had left was one reasonable option: go to the bank and use the money I'd been avoiding. I knew my dad had left me some, as a lawyer had told my mother and me in the days after he passed, but I'd never gone to claim it. Leaving it in the bank made it feel like he was still alive in a way. I didn't know how the process would work, but I was sure I could figure it out. As for what Thomas had been doing exactly, that might take a little research, but he wasn't the brightest. There was no way I couldn't figure it out if he did. I made my way to the only bank in town, an old brick-and-mortar one. Walking in, I didn't know where to go, so I went to the teller and told her I needed to withdraw five hundred dollars. I doubted my dad had left me much, and the trauma of it all had made me never want to come here, but there could be a chance.

The teller typed away for a few minutes after I gave her my details and informed me I had ten grand. I looked up at her wide-eyed. "What do you mean?"

She told me my dad had an account for me with ten thousand dollars in it. This was not the outcome I'd anticipated, and I didn't need that much. I didn't know if I should be happy or sad about it. In a way, it felt wrong to take it. I asked her if I could withdraw seven hundred in cash, and she was happy to oblige.

Walking out of there, my mind kept repeating ten thousand. A good backup plan in case anything went seriously wrong. I wondered if my mother knew about this. If she did, wouldn't she have asked by now? Thoughts aside, I'd keep the money my dad left in there as a foundation, or in case this all went up in flames. Knowing I had that eased my anxiety and gave me a relief I didn't think was possible. Thank you, Dad.

Now with my seven hundred, all I had to do was spend it on something to get me connected to the internet. I walked over to the electronics store and bought a laptop. When I was walking, it hit me that I didn't even have internet at home. I'd have to use my computer at the library or anywhere with Wi-Fi. Not convenient in the least.

Going in wasn't hard. Their stock was barely complete, and all I asked for was something that could connect to the internet. The guy running the store brought out a regular-looking laptop that he said ran everything smoothly. Looking it over, I knew it would do and would only run me two hundred.

"A year's warranty on that thing, too," he told me, pointing at it like it was a nice car. I nodded and handed him the money. I paid, left, and headed to the library.

This was not my first choice, and as with any backup plan, you have to improvise. I went around the library to a corner and tucked myself into it so people couldn't see what I was doing. I felt strange, though, like eyes might be on me. An eighteen-year-old with a brand-new laptop? I felt like people would notice, and I looked up. To my surprise, nobody was even glancing in my direction. With my paranoia out of the way, I had to get to work.

I knew I'd have to find out how to do what Thomas had been doing. I'd used the internet at school, but never cared about it as much as some of the other boys my age. Random searches, like how people buy drugs, kept leading me to one keyword. Darknet. This is what I'd focus on, as there had to be something there. Users on forums said you had to convert your money and buy it there. I didn't know how that would work, but I downloaded the necessary tools to get on it.

Browsing through the darknet was slow, and when I hit the homepage of the site I was looking for, I made sure nobody was around me in the library. It was unlimited access to drugs at the cheapest prices I'd ever seen. I could buy five hundred Xanax for only three hundred dollars. Reading up on it, I'd seen people warn that using your bank details on the website was a risk, but I had nothing to lose. I put my information in for a direct deposit and waited for the site to redirect me.

I checked out, and it seemed I needed to enter my address, name, and state. I wondered how I wouldn't simply get scammed. I pictured them sending me a picture of Xanax instead of the actual thing. I couldn't lose any money. Not in the position I was in. Browsing the forum more, I learned the site held the money until I confirmed receipt of the product. Perfect. Closing out everything, I walked home, head held high, a mission underway.

Laws

Nothing ever went right in my life for some time, leading me to believe I was cursed. Within that period, I began to theorize that the worse things that happened to me, the better things would happen in equal measure. I called it "Michael's Law" as a joke. When I was getting the mail the following week, the law I'd created finally manifested itself.

I brought my package inside, unwrapped it, and went through multiple layers, knowing exactly what was in it. I finally got to the clear bag and read the white bars printed through the see-through package that was the last layer of defense. X-A-N-A-X. Perfectly placed on the pill and on every imprint to make it look as professional as possible.

I had five hundred pills and two hundred dollars to my name. This was the start of something great, I thought. Placing the pills into a container and gently tucking them into my drawer, I stared at them for a while. Going back over to it, I opened the container and took one. I deserve it. Just one. I put the rest back and assumed that Trey wouldn't know one pill was missing, or I could just sell fewer.

I went to my bed and lay down, feeling the effects of the pill. Everything around me seemed not to matter, and I felt like I was in heaven. I found myself saying random things until I closed my eyes and let my brain wander. My body sank into the bed, and everything went dark.

When I awoke, I didn't understand what had happened at first, so I checked my phone for the time. It was a quarter to eight, and I was going to be late for school. Pain nagged at me as I weighed the pros and cons of going. School didn't matter much, but it was my last year, and I wanted to graduate and be done with it.

Letting my rationality come back to me, I packed my bags and headed downstairs, but turned back to grab a pill from my drawer, which I slipped into my wallet. Going to school was fun. In my first period, I had to read from my journal, and other than Lily ignoring me, something else at school had caught my attention.

Nicole had started to talk to me when I was out of class, and I figured I'd finally made a friend. She'd ask me things like why I wrote the things I did in my journal and what I wanted to do after this year. I told her so many times I had no clue, but she'd always joke with me and say, "It's in there somewhere. You just don't know it yet."

Sometimes, when I found myself talking to Nicole during those days, I'd think I was talking to Lily. Sitting back and relaxing felt so familiar that I had to stop myself from calling her Lily multiple times. Luckily, I'd always caught myself. I enjoyed her company, and she had high aspirations for life, which I liked.

The following week, when I was due to meet with Trey, I brought four hundred pills, as I'd begun taking some myself to help with my anxiety. Why not reap the benefits of my money and hard work, I'd think to myself as I took them from my drawer. When I showed up and waited at the water tower, Trey had been blown away by the Xanax I'd brought and the quantity.

"We'll do twelve hundred for four hundred pills. Three a pop."

Trey had told me this, biting into one. I told him this was fair and watched him produce a wad of bills and hand them to me. As he walked off, all he said was, "Same time. Three weeks from now."

I yelled back, okay.

I couldn't help but feel incredibly excited. If only Lily could see me now. I was solving problems and making money. I'd be able to buy anything I wanted and help my mother out. When I got home, I took a pill and laid all the money on the floor and just stared at it. I'd never known the feeling of having money and had no idea what to do with it. I could go out to eat, see a movie, or buy any bike I wanted. For once, I wished I had friends.

This cycle continued for the next couple of months. Selling to Trey. Putting the money away, and some in my wallet. Putting the pills away, and some in my pocket. I didn't realize I was becoming addicted until one day Nicole was talking to me at lunchtime and looked at me a couple of times. My class before had been a physics lecture, and I'd taken a Xanax on top of the one from the morning. I couldn't remember if I'd taken two or one that morning, but Nicole knew something was wrong and asked me why I was falling asleep in the middle of the day.

I combed my hands through my hair. "Work is hard, you know."

She took this as a lie and looked at me again, concerned. "You can barely keep your eyes open and you're slurring your words, Mikey."

I told her not to worry. We only had one period left.

"Alright, but please let me know if you're going
through something. I'm here for you."

Her words were lost on me, as I'd noticed Lily walking
in the schoolyard plaza with her blonde hair glowing. I
mumbled something like a thank you to Nicole and got up.

Walking over to Lily, I was high out of my mind and
didn't care what she'd say to me. When I got closer, I saw
that her eyes were bloodshot and her pupils were huge.
This stopped me, and her friend came over to ask, "What
do you want?"

I shook my head and turned away. "Forget it."

Was Lily doing drugs now? I wandered back to Nicole,
but before I reached her, the bell rang and she left in a
hurry.

Whatever. Fuck all this. I left school out the front gate
and went home, taking another pill, staring at my
bedroom ceiling. I had all the money a kid my age could
want and all the pills. I'd keep it up and earn more money.
Everything was going well for me. Michael's Law had
finally come into effect and had no signs of reverting to
the mean.

A Great Life

Walking to school with money in my pocket. I'd been
feeling good for once in my life. Trey and I had been
working together for months. My money had been coming
in better, and my addiction had worsened. I was taking
one every time I woke up and a pill every two to three
hours. In the last six months, I'd been a model student,
doped up on all the drugs I'd been taking. All the money

I'd been making was finally put to use helping my mother with the house. Funny enough, she never questioned where I got it. She just told me to keep working hard. Believe that, Mother. I will.

Something strange had happened one week during one of my drop, James looked at me for a brief moment, then away again. It was enough to alert me. I'd always picked up on social cues, and this one definitely felt like something.

I went up to him and asked if anything was wrong.

"No, you just reminded me of," he paused, "nah, it's nothing."

What did that mean? Did I remind him of himself dealing drugs? I certainly hoped not. "Well, what do I remind you of? It must be something."

James looked annoyed and told me to shut it. "I say shit on accident sometimes. Mixed you up with another kid. That's all."

I took his word for it, but the interaction was strange. Anyway, it didn't matter. I was here for a transaction. Nothing more, nothing less.

I remained committed to living my normal life the best I could and selling drugs to Trey on the side. I think school had become bearable for me since I had started taking the Xanax. The weight of getting a job and my house being taken off had also been lifted off my shoulders.

During school, English was my favorite class. I'd be high out of my mind and get to read my journal entries. We weren't required to read them aloud, but I always volunteered. I thought it was funny, and I also wanted people to notice me. I'd seen more people wanting to be my friends, and Nicole, a girl I'd met, had started to like me.

Mr. Wright started class, and as usual, I raised my hand to read my journal entry.

"Mr. Ren, it is always a pleasure to hear your entries. Start us off."

I stood up and read my latest. "I seem to dislike myself. I work on myself day by day, and even if I can improve a little, I think I'm making a positive change in my life. I've made my mother happier, which I never dreamed of doing, and in turn that made me happier. Whenever my mind tells me that I hate myself, I try to think of things I've done and will do that can help me overcome that mindset. I promise I'll get out of it."

With that, I sat down. Mr. Wright replied, "Thank you. That was very personal and brave to share with the class. Do we have anyone next who'd like to go?"

I looked to the seat in front of me, but Lily wasn't there. I'd tried my best after that day to get over her, but I couldn't. Trying to get in contact with her was useless, and last I heard, she was dating some senior. She'd stopped coming to class most days, and when she did, she looked high out of her mind.

I didn't talk to her or attempt to in those moments. She'd left me in my most vulnerable state. I'd see her sneak glances at me, and I thought it was funny. I could still hear her voice. "We are done."

If you wanted to be done, so be it, Lily. I'd taken your idea and made it better in every way.

Still, down in the very core of my existence, the part I hated and resented, I unconditionally loved her. I wanted to talk to her and tell her that what she was doing was hurting her, and I could help. I wanted her to hold me. I wanted to watch her sleep again. I wanted her in every way possible. But my mind knew that talking to her in any circumstance could be bad, as she'd threatened the police against me before.

I'd have to deal with her later. English was done, and I headed towards my other classes. I kept my pills in my wallet now. I'd finally had enough money to buy one, and it was the perfect place to keep them. Taking my beloved Xanax, I felt heavenly through the rest of my classes. And just like that, I'd traveled back in time, and school was out.

I was walking home, but higher than usual, and decided on something incredibly dumb. When I passed her house, I stopped. I couldn't move. I wanted to see her, learn about her life. In that moment, as I turned towards her door, I decided that love was the worst thing in the world. I had no control over my actions. I rang the doorbell and waited.

The idea of walking away disappeared because Katrina answered the door immediately and gave me a warm smile.

"Michael. How nice of you to visit. Come in."

I didn't know what I was doing, but I stepped in and carefully took off my shoes. This house had once been a place I loved and cherished, and it had vanished from my mind. The realization of how long it had been started to set in. Due to the pills, I wasn't anxious. I just felt a sense of eeriness.

"Would you like a Coke or water?" She was near the fridge. I told her a Coke would do and sat down at the table in the kitchen. "I haven't seen much of you and Lily lately." She looked pained as she said this.

"I barely see Lily anymore." I thought this over and told her that I hadn't seen her either, and she was probably busy with high school and the demands of being a teenager.

She shook her head. "No, I think it's much worse. I wish I could help her, but she never talks to me."

Sitting there, I knew she would ask me for help.

"But enough about me. How are you and your mother holding up?" Answering this was a breeze since I barely had to lie. I told her all about how I had a "job" now and was helping to pay for the house. Katrina smiled.

"I'm glad at least one teenager I know is being responsible."

Ironic. I took a drink.

"Yes, I've been trying my hardest. With my dad gone, I feel like it's my responsibility to step up. And you've always been a second mother to me, so maybe I could help Lily."

I wanted to help Lily for my own sake, but benefiting her and sharing this information would lead me to more details, which is precisely what I needed. Katrina stared at her drink for a while before speaking.

"All I know is she's been around a boy much older than her. I think his name is Lucas, and I've never met him. Do you know him?"

I shook my head.

"I know they're doing drugs together, and I've tried to confront her about it, but she never..." She went silent. I looked up. "I get it. Not fully as a parent, but I understand how hard it must be. I can try my best to talk to her this week."

Katrina looked happy for a brief moment before going back to staring at her cup. "Thank you, Michael. That means a lot." Anytime, I told her.

I felt I'd overstayed my welcome, and right on time, my phone started to ring.

"Thank you for having me over. I'll be back soon. I promise."

I headed to the door, phone still ringing. Katrina didn't move from the table. She mustered up a thank you, and I was off.

As soon as I was out, I flipped open my phone. "Yo."
The voice on the other end started to laugh.

"Is that how you start every conversation with a girl?"

Getting out of the house so quickly, I'd assumed James or Trey was calling me. This was Nicole. This was unexpected.

"I don't receive many calls from girls. Sorry. What's up, Nicole?"

Why in the world was she calling me? I had to be suspicious in every regard ever since Thomas had been put in the hospital, and this was no exception. She replied casually and asked if I was free tonight. There would be a party downtown. I hated parties, but maybe I could find Lily there, I thought.

"Yeah, a party sounds fun. Just text me the time and where to meet."

Nicole sounded very excited to hear this. "Okay, I'll do just that. You better not flake."

The line went dead.

Now I had two women who needed me to do something. I had to go to a party and be aware of the police, and I had to find information on Lily and Lucas. I needed to stop by my house and prep. Ever since I started working with Trey, my life had been much better. I always had money. My mother still drank, which bothered me, but once someone hits the bottle, they never stop. Was I turning into that? As I walked home, my mind wandered.

Planning Dates

I'd finally reached home when I came back to my senses. My mind was always wandering back in time. Maybe that was my punishment for what I'd done to Thomas. To always be trapped in memories was hell. Getting into my house, I grabbed a couple of twenties from my drawer and a knife. A sharp one I'd acquired from one of my deals with Trey.

"Need something to protect yourself with all those drugs you're keeping on you," he'd said as he played with the blade. I remembered him sticking it in the ground next to me. "Keep it."

Walking home with it, I'd wondered if he'd used it on someone, which I had nearly done. I needed to be prepared. Before leaving, I decided to check on my mother. Knocking on her door, I told her I was coming in. She was in bed, a book next to her with a name I couldn't make out, and her oxycontin. "Mikey," she said in a raspy tone. I wanted to make this quick.

"I left the payment for the house this month on the table. I'm going out tonight with a girl."

She had no emotion in her at all. I thought a parent would be a little more surprised if their child said that outright to them.

She looked over and coughed. She struggled to swallow a pill, which she took with no water. "You look just like him."

I knew she was talking about my father. That was the last thing I needed to hear. Leaving the room, I told her I loved her and to take care tonight. Grabbing water, I popped two Xanax. I always kept at least ten in my wallet just in case. I needed my wits tonight. I was completely different from the first time Lily had almost inadvertently killed me. I was now grounded with confidence and pride. Checking my phone, it was about seven, and Nicole had told me to meet her near the football field at our school. It was a fifteen-minute walk, but I didn't want to stay in the house longer than I had to.

The conditions outside were nice. I wished I had a cigarette, a habit I'd picked up from Trey. I could hear his voice. "Only Luckies. I like my luck."

Since I had time, I decided to stop by the gas station. I walked over and asked for a pack of Lucky Strikes. The cashier eyed me. "You don't look old enough to be eighteen."

I told her I was nineteen and got that a lot. Seemingly, my lie was good enough, or she didn't care, as I paid my six dollars. Five for the smokes, one for a lighter. Lighting up a cigarette, I headed to the football field.

I didn't think Nicole knew I took any drugs or smoked, or maybe that's just what I wanted to believe. Whenever we talked, it was about school or what was happening in town. Taking a drag, my mind wandered to the past, which I blocked immediately. I needed to focus. I felt cursed as I walked along. My thoughts swirled around my head as if I were watching stars speed around the sun. I wished the incessant thinking would end.

The party would be hazardous for me. If the police showed up, I didn't want to be there. They'd already questioned Thomas's friends, but my name had never come up. I assumed Lily hadn't said anything, but only she would know. My phone beeped with a text: See you soon. It was 7:45. I threw my cigarette and crushed it with my shoe. Thank God for the wind. I wouldn't smell like a smoker, I hoped. I was already there but decided to walk around the school. The wind felt lovely, blowing my hair, making my sweater toss and turn. Maybe I'd write about the wind in my next journal entry. It's always traveling past so many souls and seeing everything, yet we are oblivious to it.

Being almost eight, I walked back to the front of the field and saw her standing there. I stopped for a moment to assess the situation. She looked anxious, fidgeting with her sweater straps. I'd always been bad with girls besides Lily. I couldn't understand them, and when I tried to help and fix their problems, it always seemed to backfire. Maybe the problem was me, but Nicole could be different. As she started to walk over, she saw me and waved, which made my stomach flutter a little. I realized I hadn't felt that way since Lily. Should I be with Lily right now? I needed to do something at least.

I greeted her, and she was dressed very modestly, which I liked. Skater pants, a black hoodie, and some Nikes. I complimented her on it, and she smiled and told me this was her usual outfit. I told her we had that in common. As we walked over to the party, I made small talk, but I didn't let my mind drift. I needed to be careful and on guard at all times. I'd formed a plan to find Lily. Assuming this was a party, her boyfriend would be here, and if I could get Lily alone for five minutes, I could explain. "We're here, Mikey," Nicole said, gesturing towards the house. I thought in my head too much. I played it off and told her let's get started. I thought it wouldn't be crowded because of the emptiness outside, but inside was a different story. People passed me left and right, drinks in one hand, smokes in the other. If I'm Lily, where would I be? I needed to focus on Nicole first. My mind was a mess.

"Nicole, let's grab some drinks," I told her over my shoulder. When we went over to the table to get some, I was able to get a Xanax down with mine. I knew that combination could kill me, so I only took two sips.

Nicole watched me and asked what we should do. I wished I could be normal and say something like "have fun with you," but no, I was a moron too busy worrying about a girl who didn't love me and the police. I swore I could see Thomas's friends look in my direction as I thought that. Reminder to self: don't go to parties. I brushed it off and told her let's settle in. She was already drinking, and I saw her friend group in the corner of the living room. If I could get her over there, maybe she'd forget about me. I started walking in that direction and told her I was going to look for some downers upstairs. People at parties always sell upstairs, so I knew that's where I could find Lily. Nicole frowned and told me to stay with her for a bit, but I insisted.

"I'll get some for you too. I promise," I told her with a smile.

I felt terrible doing this to her. She was a nice girl. Why did I do this to myself? I passed all the people on the stairs. The smoke clouded over me and smelled like a mix of strawberries and beer. I needed to find an opiate dealer, and it would lead me to them. Suddenly, I was rudely interrupted as a boy my age, whom I recognized as Connor, pushed me into the wall. I didn't have time for this nonsense.

"I know what you did, and I'm going to make you hurt. You stole our business from us," he said, looking like he wanted to murder me. What did he know? For all I knew, he could be talking about anything. I told him he'd had a little too much to drink, which got me a nice right hook to the face.

I could taste blood in my mouth. I wanted to fight him, but with the Xanax, I had no energy, and the last thing I needed was for the police to find out I'd fought one of Thomas's friends. I walked down the hall as he gave me a good "Go fuck yourself." My jaw hurt so badly. For the first time, I wished I could change these benzos into Advil. Then it hit me, just not a punch this time. I needed painkillers for actual pain. Thank you, Connor, you fucking moron. You've helped me out.

Walking to the end of the hallway, I entered what I assumed to be the master bedroom to see a bunch of couples on one side and others doing drugs on the other. I needed to find Lily's boyfriend. If I could get his contact information and build a rapport, I could take the necessary steps.

In this room, I felt entirely out of place. It was dreamlike. More of a nightmare or fever dream, as I saw so many things that shouldn't be happening, happening. I tried to avert my eyes from what was going on to the left and stumbled towards the right, where I saw people with needles. Was heroin what she'd resorted to? I could barely think straight. I'd thought she'd been smoking weed and getting high like every other teenager. How could she have spiraled this far? I had to fix this.

Stumbling forward, I saw what I thought was her. Her blonde hair and body sprawled against someone I could only assume was him. She didn't seem to be awake, which worried me, but her boyfriend was talking to two others when I finally reached him. For an odd moment, our eyes met, and I felt like the look in mine could kill right then and there. Then again, I was so out of it I didn't even know if my face was corresponding with my brain.

"You looking to buy?" he asked casually. This was the first time I'd heard him speak. He sounded out of it, but still in reality.

I needed to pull my trump card. Looking at him casually, I said, "I've got some Xanax pills I've been trying to sell here, but no one's been talking to me. We could trade them if you want."

God, that sounded much better in my head, but I had no clue about the price of opiates, and I needed him to take the bait. He mouthed my sentence back to himself without words and told me to show him what I had. I thought at least ten pills would be worth however much heroin goes for. The sudden realization that maybe I should have done more research hit me hard. Failure.

No. I couldn't quit now. He took the pills I was holding up and popped one immediately with no water. I could tell he was tasting it to check if it was real, because the fake ones aren't bitter. I was in luck, as mine were.

"Ten for how much?" he said, looking up. He liked them. Again, I didn't know prices, so I offered up a knuckleball. "However much you think is fair."

He nodded and pulled out a tube that was about a quarter full and gave it to me. All of this was happening too fast, and nothing had gone wrong yet, which was slowly rotting my brain. Failure. "This should be plenty fair for ten," he said, looking down at Lily. Lily. I'd forgotten why I was here. I needed to know this was him. I moved closer and sat down next to his group.

"I'm Michael, by the way. If you want to buy more, I can sell to you cheap anytime."

He looked me over again, up and down. I felt like a dog at the pound while people decided if I was good enough to be adopted. I hated this. "Lucas," he muttered while combing his hair. "And I'll buy more off you tonight for real money once she wakes up." He gestured towards Lily's lifeless body.

I needed more information on this. She looked dead to me, and my mind kept picturing her dead. I thought of Thomas, his bloody body, what I'd done. I started to have a panic attack.

"Yeah, tonight. Here's my number. I just, I don't know, I have to go see my girl. Just text me when you want to buy," was all I could get out before I stumbled out of the room. I snatched up whatever Xanax I had left in my wallet, which was two, and swallowed them. I needed to think. I couldn't be here right now. If I could get to Nicole, she'd understand.

Going down the stairs, I spotted Nicole in the corner. Alone. Failure. I'd fucked up. She must hate me. I missed a step but caught myself. God, I'd taken so many drugs and had so many on me. If the police showed up. My mind was a mess, and I kept seeing dead people. I needed to get to Nicole. She saw me coming over and didn't say a word. I collapsed onto her and held on. My brain hurt. I wanted the pain to go away, but it wouldn't. The Xanax I'd taken wasn't working, and it felt like a knife was stuck in me, hurting me over and over.

I didn't want to open my eyes. I didn't want to face Nicole. I wanted to disappear. Failure. Failure. Failure. I opened my eyes and asked her if she could walk me out of here. Hesitantly, she obliged and propped me up, and we walked out. The air felt so much better outside. The noise was gone, and I almost felt happy for a second as we walked down the street, until we stopped.

"Why did you leave?"

Nicole let go of me, and I stood against a fence near the sidewalk. I didn't know how to respond. "I want to know why you left me," she asked again. I couldn't tell if she was hurt or mad, or both. My head hurt so much I needed her to hold me. I watched as she came up and pushed me. "Are you mute now, Mikey? You left me. Alone. And now you won't speak to me."

My phone buzzed. Could it be Lucas? I took a gamble and guessed it was, because the only other person who texted me was Nicole.

I mustered up some courage, despite my brain being fried. "I left to go check on a friend, and I got us a double date for after the party."

Nicole looked at me, puzzled. I was waiting for her to backhand the shit out of me, but it never came. She walked around and asked me to explain.

"This guy I met, I think his name is Lucas, is dating my old friend and wants to meet up later."

Now I felt like the slap. She got close to me. "This isn't a fucking double date. It's about drugs, isn't it?"

I was tired of lying, so I nodded in defeat.

I watched as she put her head in her hands and then regained her composure. I was almost impressed by how fast she did that.

"You know, if I didn't have the stupidest fucking crush on you, I would hate you. But for some fucking reason, part of me, some stupid fucking part, is actually telling me to go with you."

Well, I thanked "that part" in my mind and told her to trust me. I'd make up for tonight. She settled for a fine and sat down against the fence, and I did too. I reached out to hold her hand, and she didn't pull away. I stared into the distance and told her, "The night is still young. I'll make it up to you, Nicole. I promise."

I don't know how long Nicole and I sat there, but it felt nice. To feel the wind against my skin, to look at the moon, and mostly to hold her hand. I'd never considered the possibility of falling for Nicole, but perhaps at that moment, I'd started to.

While we sat there, I pulled out my phone and saw a text from a number I assumed was his. @2 stadium dugout, it read. I had roughly two hours until then, which meant I needed a plan. Talking to Lily alone and appealing to her was a long shot, and I didn't like to take risks, so I ruled that out. Fighting Lucas would only end with my teeth being kicked in and me being arrested, so that was ruled out. I hated thinking, so I put it off by staring at the sky.

I saw two stars lined up completely parallel to each other. One was bigger than the other, but the other was brighter. I didn't know my stars, and I didn't know if this was even normal, but suddenly it clicked for me. The stars would align in my favor tonight. I'd been shown the playing field was even, and I knew what I had to do.

That time was still an hour off, and Nicole slumped onto my shoulder.

"You know, Mikey, this is all I ever wanted from tonight. I have a lot of friends, but I hate parties. I just wanted an excuse to be with you."

I squeezed her hand and told her I wished I'd known, so I could have made it better. Before letting her speak, I pointed out the stars I'd seen.

"You see the two stars aligned next to each other?"

She nodded against my shoulder.

"You're the one who's extremely bright. You always look for the best in people and never let things get you down."

This gave her a laugh. "How would you know that?"

I told her the way she'd acted tonight had shown me that.

She spoke in my ear, almost as if pointing towards the bigger star. "That one doesn't shine. You were planning to tell me that's you."

I mustered up a laugh and told her she'd read me like a book.

"Maybe we're both the bright star, Mikey. We don't have to be separate. In this moment, right now, we are together, and we shine as bright as that star."

Her words felt like poetry to me, and without knowing how to respond, still out of it, I turned towards her and kissed her. I'd never felt such a wonderful feeling. My stomach felt fuzzy. We were both stars. Nicole looked at me dreamily and fell into my lap with a smile on her face.

Instead of overthinking this whole plan, I should spend the rest of the night with Nicole. I'd always heard love was a positive feeling, but never imagined it on this level. Why not just call it off and forget about Lily? Failure. No. I had a job to do. Nicole couldn't be around for it, or else she'd hate me until the end of time. I had to play my part.

I pulled my phone out and read 1:20. I had to get moving. I looked at Nicole, who was falling asleep on my lap, and told her to let me walk her home, to which she happily agreed if I held her hand. The walk wasn't far, only about seven blocks, which would take about twenty minutes. The stadium would be about three blocks from there, so I'd arrive with plenty of time.

Hit

Dropping Nicole off was simple, as I didn't want to account for her in this plan I had to come up with. The fewer things in the plan, the less that could go wrong. When I reached her house, I said bye, gave her a hug, and went on my way. The streetlights would guide me to the stadium.

I hadn't been to the stadium much, as I didn't like going to sporting events. Even though it was my last year at school, I'd never felt like I belonged. Sometimes I'd go with acquaintances and always feel awkward. Sitting around on the bleachers, my mind couldn't focus on the game. It only focused on the people around me. Usually they'd all move around, leaving me alone. The last one I'd gone to, I'd left entirely when that happened and walked around town.

The thing I liked about this town was how close everything was together. People always hated that, though. They wanted to leave and had aspirations for the big city and talked incessantly about it, which annoyed me. Most of the time, I wasn't in the conversation, just a listener, and it annoyed me. Why would someone want to be surrounded by a vast city and so many people? I'd always wondered.

As my mind dragged on, I stopped to light up a cigarette. I didn't know if they relieved stress, but I always felt more confident with one. I always imagined myself as a Clint Eastwood type. Cigarette in mouth, revolver in the other hand. I hated the addiction, but not for the reasons most do. I couldn't stand the smell, and I hated that other people could smell it on me. Tonight, though, that would be the least of my worries.

Arriving at the stadium, I had to climb a simple metal fence to walk over to the dugout. As I knew I'd be coming here, I had to assess my mental state. I didn't have anxiety due to the pills, and the alcohol hadn't killed me, so I assumed I was in the clear. If I could make it through tonight and get home, I felt like everything in the world would be better. Sometimes I had these notions that if I planned something so meticulously and it worked in my head, I already knew how I'd feel afterwards. It might be a side effect of benzos, but if not, at least it was there to comfort me. "Rookie," I heard him call out from the dugout. Interestingly enough, he was lined up near the left of the dugout, directly below the bigger star. From where I was standing, I was in front of the shining star I'd seen with Nicole. I could take this as a good omen. I waved to him with three fingers, came up to the dugout entrance, and entered from the side. There was a long bench where all the baseball players would sit, and he sat at the end with Lily on his lap.

This didn't shock me the way I'd expected it to. It was clear they were connected on some level I didn't understand, but I knew it was wrong. I took my seat near Lily's legs and looked over. I didn't bother using his name, and I doubted he even remembered mine. His eyes were glossed over, and he was tying his arm up. He called me rookie again, and I looked up at him.

"Say we trade three grams of heroin for twenty Xanax?"

I still didn't know prices, so I had to tell him these were 2mg and worth more than that. He dully looked at me, like a person waking up from bed. "I got some percs I can add onto it."

Painkillers. This could be all I needed to finish this. I asked him to show them to me, and he went into his pocket and pulled out a bag. He tossed it over for me to examine. Looking at the white pills and sneaking a glance at Lily, I asked, "How do I know these are legit?"

Surprisingly, he responded with, "Same goes for you."

I got up and handed him my Xanax. Lily looked to be asleep and at peace, which made me more confident. "Let's both try them out. Three each. I promise you these are the best you can find," I told him. I wasn't sure how painkillers would affect me, but to win at something, you have to take a risk.

Looking at me quizzically, he nodded and took the three. I looked over at him again and asked if he could show me how to use the heroin. He laughed at this and said, "First, don't say it like that. You don't 'use the heroin.' You have to do this." I knew he was already shooting up when I arrived, but I needed him to continue. "You take this," he said, showing me the needle, "and find the best vein where your arm is wrapped." He injected the heroin into himself at that point.

I thanked him, and he passed me the needle. I hadn't taken the painkillers yet, which he was oblivious to, but there was no way I was going to do this.

"Here's the liquid rock. Trust me, this shit will knock you. Just look at her," he said, motioning to Lily.

I held the needle in my hand. "Oh, I bet it will."

I paused for a moment. "How much have you had to drink tonight?"

I asked in a carefree manner. He paused. "Some vodka and this and that. Why do you ask?"

I looked down and didn't answer. He repeated his question.

I stared off at the baseball field to reply. "Don't you think you have too many things in your system? Like, drinks, heroin, Xanax?"

Startled by this, he looked up. "Xanax wouldn't affect me in any way, no?"

"Well, if you took three at once while actively shooting heroin, it could have an effect. Just a thought."

I could tell he was starting to get angry. He tried to get up and fell against the gate in front of him. I walked over and looked him in the eyes.

"Scared?" I asked in a taunting tone. I could tell he was trying to speak, but no words came out. I checked my phone. 2:18 a.m. The drugs had all kicked in. He would overdose, and Lily was knocked out, and only I could save him.

Again, knowing he could hear me but not respond, I pulled out a cigarette and lit it.

"I knew you'd take the pills, and I knew what it would do. You see, I know a druggie because I am one. The only difference is I take mine to stay alive. You take yours for fun. But with fun comes risks. And with risks can come death. An accidental overdose."

He looked petrified, and I went over to Lily and propped her up against the wall.

"I'll be here until it's over. Goodbye, Lucas."

I pulled out my phone again and waited. I got a text from Nicole that read, I can't sleep, can you talk? After this was done, yes, Nicole, we could talk. I walked over to him again and examined him as he stared at me, unable to move. I hadn't touched him, and this would surely be ruled as a simple accidental overdose. Freeing Lily from this person and getting rid of someone I despised so much.

After drifting off into my thoughts, he began to seize. I knew this was possible from an overdose at that dosage. It was disturbing to watch. He started to throw up and was able to turn over to keep himself from choking.

"I've got to hand it to you. I don't know if it's your conscience, probably not, but your body still wants to live."

He seized in motions that a human would be disgusted by. The body moving so fast and so unnaturally was not a pretty sight. Finally, with one last tick, it stopped.

I couldn't go over to check for a pulse, since that would place me here, and a fingerprint on that area would be impossible to explain. I rolled my sweater over my hand and put it on his heart, but nothing. He could still be alive, but I doubted anyone would find him until tomorrow, or at least until Lily woke up. I decided he was dead and had to choose whether to leave her here or carry her home.

If I chose the latter, I'd be a moron. But I didn't want her to have to see this. To go through more pain. To get in trouble with her mother and the school. I felt horrible for her. I spoke aloud. "I promise I'll make this up to you."

I felt her hand and placed it in her sweater pocket, and promptly left.

Not thinking of what I'd just done, I needed to go somewhere. My father had always taken me to Lake Leslie, which was just a couple of blocks away. He'd always wanted me to be good at fishing and would lecture me about being safe and how I'd ever survive in the wild. I remember telling him I wouldn't have a fishing pole in the wild, to which he laughed.

I'd climbed over the gate and been walking there on autopilot. I had no clue why I was thinking of my father and fishing after what had just happened. I knew I could get there and rest. When I was rested, I could think about what to do next. Leslie was almost always deserted except for older people in town who liked to fish or high school students looking for a place to get high. I was sure there would be no one at this hour, and I needed complete silence.

With my brain not shutting up, I finally reached the outer edge of the lake and slammed my fist into a tree. My stomach turned, nauseous, and everything hurt. I stumbled into the tiny forest opening and fell. I kept thinking about what I'd just done and threw up. I wanted to disappear. I wanted the pain to end. I asked God in my head to make it stop, but it only got worse. I crawled to the nearest rock and rolled up into a fetal position and started to cry. What was happening to my body? I'd never felt this intense pain in my life. It wasn't like being stabbed. It was like my cells deteriorating and killing me.

Rolling over, I looked towards the lake, which reflected the sky. I saw the stars in it and knew they'd granted me a saving grace. Using all my energy, I opened my phone and called Nicole. When she answered, she was cheerful and said hi like normal, but I couldn't speak. I began to sob, which started to worry her. I had to tell her where I was. I needed someone to hold me. I wanted someone to hold me. Finding my voice over her worried talk, I told her I was at the lake, and she said she'd come get me and hung up.

Whenever my father was done lecturing me about fishing, I'd always skip rocks. It was one of the only things that amazed him because he couldn't do it, no matter how many times I tried to help.

"You hold it with these fingers and flick your wrist," I'd say while slinging one across the lake. I'd always get over ten skips. He'd pick one up, look it over like a foreign object, then proceed to skip it once before it fell into the water.

With the rock in my hand, I flung it across the lake. Splash. No skips. I found another one. Flung it as best I could. Same result. Defeated, I fell and started to cry again, talking aloud. "Father, where are you when I need you?"

Why wasn't he here to help me? I hated everything: my parents, my friends, my school, my town, and most of all, I hated my putrid self. My father's own life had ended, and it caused my mother to self-destruct and me to change. What would be the repercussions of his death? Of what I'd done to Thomas? What had I become?

"Michael?" I heard softly behind me. Nicole stood there looking at me with a saddened expression, very different from the one she'd had just two hours ago. I got to my feet and told her I needed her to take me home. She didn't ask any questions and nodded. "It's only right if I return the favor."

When we got to her car, I closed the door and put my head on the window while the radio played. We didn't talk, but the radio did in the silence. Bohemian Rhapsody

came on, and that song about a man confessing to his
mother what he'd done filled the car. I stared out the
window and let the words wash over me.

Dreams

After that night, I didn't leave my room all of Sunday.
I fretted about school coming up, even though there were
only two weeks left. I'd graduate and do whatever I
wanted from there. My body had calmed down after I'd
taken my pills, and I was able to purchase more with the
laptop I'd bought. Trey would need a new delivery soon,
so I'd bought a thousand pills for an insane five hundred
and fifty-seven dollars.

Walking over to my mirror, I ran my hand through my
thin brown hair. It was getting longer, which I liked, and I
wanted to look my best. I'd decided I needed to take
things more seriously with graduation and all. I had to
step up in my father's absence, and I'd already lost
whatever innocence I might've had left.

My mother stopped to check in on me. She gave a
light knock, and I let her know it was okay to come in. She
looked in much better spirits lately and had been walking
around the house and going outside, which made me feel
better. At least I was helping one person. She looked
around the room and at the sun outside. "Mikey, you're
always so busy. Are you taking the day off today?"

It was true. I was practically never home anymore. I
told her I was nervous about graduation and a little
depressed. Hearing this, she walked over to my bed and
sat down.

"I'm sorry to have burdened you like this at such a young age, Mikey. I know you must feel depressed. But I'm always going to be here for you from now on."

She hugged me and told me she was proud of me for having a job and graduating. I thanked her, and she told me she'd let me be and left the room.

Failure. The word repeated in my head. I knew that taking the drugs Lucas had given me the night before would be a horrible idea, but anything at this point was better than the alternative. I had nothing else to do today anyway. I doubted Nicole would want to hang out, or that Lily would be home safe. I was just making excuses. I knew it. My brain was looking for any way out of what I was about to do.

My right arm had a lace around it, showing the vein. It was like watching a movie of someone else doing this. I didn't want this, so why was my body moving without my brain? My head echoed with terrible thoughts. I couldn't stop myself at this point. The physical pain, the mental pain. I was too weak to go on. All I felt was pain as the needle went through.

I didn't feel anything anymore. I relaxed against my bedframe and stared at the wall. I felt warmth inside me, the same warmth I felt when I was with Nicole, the same warmth Lily had given me when she was around. In a way, this feeling twisted, and I became out of body. Everything I stared at zoomed in and out of focus. Gone were any worries I had, and gone were any goals. It was pure bliss that overtook me, and I felt myself start to fade.

"Why don't you ever just leave me alone and trust that I can take care of myself?" A familiar voice said. I was at a diner, and there were people all around me talking, but it was all gibberish. I looked forward to see Lily standing in front of me. "So are you going to always play hero? I'm not a little girl you need to rescue."

I didn't know how to respond. How could she be here, and why was nobody paying attention? The diner shifted towards a red color in my surroundings and faded to just Lily standing in front of me.

"You always go on and on about how you need to protect me, but you never once asked me what I want in life."

She strutted around, just like how she used to when she was angry at school or at her mother.

"But oh, precious Mikey has to step in because he knows what's best for me. I'm just a doll to you."

I reached out to motion, but my hands didn't work, and all I could mutter was a soft, No, that's not right. She walked over to me, standing tall. "Then why don't you leave me alone, like I told you before. Maybe the people you think I need saving from aren't the problem."

She pointed her finger at me. "It's you."

Was I in hell, atoning for what I'd done? I buried my face in my hands. This shouldn't be happening. Pain shouldn't follow me and hurt me even more after all I'd done. I was too tired of it. All I wanted was for something to take it away, to be gone like a leaf in the wind. To be free like a bird flying away into the sky.

"Well, you're not even going to say I look good today?"

I still had my face in my hands. I didn't want to see Lily.

"I'm just joking, Michael. Here, take my hand."

Warmth grasped my hands, and I was face to face with Nicole. Finding my voice, I asked her why she was here.

"You brought me here. Or maybe I was meant to be here. I think that's up to you to decide," she said as she twirled her hair with her finger. Needing something, I asked her the only thing I could think of. "Nicole, if it's not too much, can you hold me until I go?"

She came over and embraced me like a loving partner I'd known for years. No words needed to be spoken. Everything felt at ease. She whispered to me, "Soon, I'll have to go, love."

Not wanting her to leave, I followed up. "Nicole, where are you going?"

Still holding onto me. "The real world, Michael. The one where we can be happy together."

I felt the warmth fading. Not wanting it to end, I asked one last question. "How do I find the real world?"

The words came from nobody, as she was already gone, but it was distinctly her voice: "You're called to it."

Everything was dark now. No more Lily and no more Nicole. I was sitting in darkness with no telling of the time or what would happen next. It felt as if I were in a prison of my mind, and it had no intention of letting me leave. I started to slap myself and tell my brain to wake up. This only made the place I was in start to shake, until suddenly everything transformed into a familiar place.

"Hello, son. It's been a while."

It couldn't be. I'd closed off these memories. He shouldn't exist in my brain. Not after what he did to my mother and me, I told myself.

"I know you must have built up quite a hatred of me over these past years, and I'm sorry, Michael."

I was finally able to stand up. "Bullshit," I yelled at him. "You left us here and made me go and do this. I sell drugs to keep our house. I had to hurt people because my mind is so fucked up. I'm doing heroin now because I can't cope with the fucking pain you left me. You have no goddamn right to even speak to me."

His back still faced me. He'd never turned. I didn't want to see his face anyway, as the last time I'd seen it was enough to haunt my mind forever.

He lifted his head to look through an imaginary window. "Son, did it ever occur to you that people go through all the same pain you go through? Perhaps even worse? I knew what would come of my action, but the pain was unbearable. Just like what you're doing now. You might not even wake up from this."

I had nothing to say to him. A father is supposed to protect you. If he had his pain, he should have owned up to it like a man instead of forcing it onto my mother and me.

I turned my back to walk out of the room. Anyplace but here.

"Well, Father, if I don't wake up, we can truly talk. Until that day, though, I will be a better man than you," I said as I walked into the entrance in front of me.

Everything around me began to disappear, but I heard him utter one last statement.

"The day will come when you won't be."

The sun hit my eyes, and I felt gnawing hunger all over my body that wanted something it couldn't have. I was sprawled on the floor, staring at the damn window over my bed. I still felt high, but everything that had happened felt eerily real. I got up and felt better, like my body was in the clouds and my mind was in a separate place. I felt like talking to people and wanted to hear them after that.

First, I wanted to call Katrina to see what had happened with Lily, but I decided against it. I needed to write down everything in my journal and remember everything that was said to me. My brain has always been my best tool, so I suppose it could have been trying to tell me something. As I wrote, my father's words echoed in my head nonstop. The day will come when you won't be. Did he mean not being a good father, or did he mean being a better man than him? I didn't understand and decided it wasn't worth it since they were senseless delusions I'd had while high.

I had to get my mind in order. That was what I did best. I would go to school tomorrow and finish my last two weeks. I would act completely innocent so nobody suspected me. Then I'd meet up with Trey after school and deliver the next batch to him. Those were the two things I needed done. After that, it was up to me to talk to Lily, talk to Nicole, lie in my bed, and rot.

With all these thoughts in my head, I lay back down. I wanted today to end with meaningless conversations with people who didn't exist. I grabbed a water from my nightstand with my pill bottle and took two Xanax and stared at the ceiling until I fell asleep. I will be a better man than you, Father. The day would come when I was, and I would make it happen.

Overload

Sitting in my chair waiting for class to start always felt like a luxury. I didn't want it to start, but at the same time I did. I couldn't describe the feeling. A feeling of being stuck in the middle. Daydreaming in my thoughts, Nicole tapped me on the shoulder and gave me a smile on the way to her seat. She was wearing a pretty black sweater today with white font on it. She did have good taste. I realized I was staring at her and turned away. All I could think about was what she'd said to me in that otherworldly place. The world where we can be happy together.

Would it be possible for that to happen? I'd already done so much in such little time that I felt like the whole world might crash down onto me at any given moment. The last thing I wanted to do was involve her in what I'd done two days ago. Unsurprisingly, the seat in front of me was empty. I knew she wouldn't be here today, but the dumbest part of me had imagined it last night. If I'd seen her in my hallucinations, why couldn't she be here?

"Good morning, class. As always, we'll start with the journals."

Mr. Wright brought me back to reality. Knowing I was going to have to go first was depressing. I didn't want to talk about anything I'd written down. Instinctively, Wright looked to me, and I stood up. I looked towards the front of the class and just told myself not to say anything weird.

"For my journal, I wrote about the dreams I had this weekend. In them, I was visited by people I knew, and I don't think it was sad or happy. In a way, it was seeing what would happen with them in the future. I don't know what to make of it." I sat down. My teacher was intrigued by this and told me, "Many things we see in our dreams reflect our real emotions. They simply cannot be accessed when we're awake. Thank you for going first, Michael."

Real emotions.

Walking home, I stopped by my house to pick up my package to give to Trey. I was going to get over two grand today, which on any other day would have made me ecstatic, but not today. School had been a bore, and I'd learned nothing about any death. I began to question if Lucas was even real. Maybe the Xanax had destroyed my brain and I was seeing hallucinations. I decided this was not the mindset I wanted going into a drug deal, and switched to focus.

Arriving at the water tower, which was our usual spot, Trey was there by himself this time, which was unusual. He always had Tony with him, but a rule of thumb is never to ask too many questions you probably don't want the answers to. I waved at him and came up.

"A thousand Xanax. Perfectly pressed," I said with a bit of dignity and a smile. I was genuinely proud, holding that amount of drugs in my hand. All those pills looking so beautifully white was a thing of power. Trey took them, looked them over, and reached in and bit off a half like he usually did to test them. He nodded at me.

"Listen, kid, next meeting will be a month from today. Tony got held up, and we need to keep our heads down," he said as he pulled out the cash and handed it to me.

I replied with another devious smile. "You know my opsec is the best. I won't let you down. A month from now, and I'll have another thousand for you."

He nodded, but he wasn't his usual self. I could see something was plaguing him. He started to walk off and waved a hand towards me. "Just keep your head down, kid."

I watched him go and quickly put the two thousand away without bothering to count it. I knew it was the right amount, but didn't want anyone to see me with it.

Making my way back home, I knew I could give my mother seven-fifty and use the rest on myself. I was thinking of buying a car with all the money I'd made. In the back of my mind, I kept thinking about how much more I'd have if I weren't using my own product, but whatever. I put the rest of the money in my hiding spot in the bedroom. Before leaving, I went to my dresser, took a couple of pills, put on a sweater, and headed out.

I wanted to walk all around town on the high I was feeling. I felt richer than anyone, and the drugs made me feel euphoric. There was a nagging feeling of wanting someone, but I couldn't quite put my finger on it. My phone was in my pocket so I could call Nicole, but I wanted to see Lily. All I could remember when I thought of her was what she looked like in that dugout. A dead body lying passed out on so many drugs that used to be a beautiful soul. Part of me knew I couldn't keep this image in my head, and my mind would not give it a rest. To her house I went.

Not too far away, I only had to walk a short while before arriving. To my surprise, I had a burst of anxiety I wasn't used to. I reached for my wallet to take a Xanax. I hadn't expected this, but I needed to go in now that I was here, and I was sure I'd been seen. I was surprised to see the police in two cars in front of her house. I knew I had to act like a concerned friend. What if she said something stupid about Thomas, given her current state? My mind was at a loss for how to play this.

Coming up to the gate, the officer who'd seen me came over, and I introduced myself as a family friend and gave my name. Looking at me quizzically, he turned his head. "Michael, huh? Are you a senior in high school?"

What did he want? All I could do was nod. The officer came around with a strange smile. "Your name's been coming up. A lot, actually. Someone in your grade seems to think you know more than you're letting on."

Was he looking for a reaction from me? Realizing I was zoning out, all I replied with was, "Oh. I hope everything is okay."

I don't believe he liked this and moved away from the gate so I could enter. I walked towards the house, and I swore I could feel his eyes on me.

"I forgot to introduce myself. I'm Officer Resen. We'll be in contact soon."

Move forward. I didn't say anything. I went to the nearest bathroom and turned on the fan. I threw up a few times, cleaned up my face, and took some more pills from my wallet. I saw a towel next to the shower and buried my face in it. "They're onto me," I whispered to myself. It was always in the back of my mind, but I'd never fully allowed it in my head. If they knew about Thomas, which I was sure he meant, did he know anything about Lily's boyfriend? I needed to see her. I got up, but barely could. I looked in the mirror and saw my light brown hair all a mess from the wind, and buried it in the towel. My pupils were huge, and the mirror seemed to black out my face. I couldn't see who I was anymore. What I'd done was real. Not a dream.

Praying nobody would see me, I left the downstairs bathroom and headed upstairs to her bedroom. I knocked three times. "I told you, I don't know anything," a voice said. She thought I was the police or her mom. I needed to tell her it was me, but I hadn't truly spoken to her in months. What could I possibly say?

"Michael. It's me, Michael."

No response. I leaned against the door with my head until I almost fell forward when it opened. "You look terrible," was all she said as she stared right at me. It hurt so bad, but I did look terrible, inside and out. Everything I'd done had made me a horrible human being. Lily was the only person who even knew how awful a person I could be.

"Well, have you gone mute in the last couple of months? It's rude to come into a girl's room and not say anything," she said in a sarcastic voice, looking ready to slap me if I didn't speak.

I fell to my knees in front of her and started to cry.

"I'm sorry. I'm so sorry. For everything." That was all I could muster. She watched this unfold without saying a word. Perhaps she didn't know what I was apologizing for, as I'd done so many things wrong. All I knew was that in that moment, I needed her, and I had to get something off my chest. The interaction with the cop and everything that had happened over the week had been too much. "Get up," she said, motioning over to the side of her bed.

"What are you even apologizing for? You look like you just killed my father or something."

I wanted to throw up again when she said the word killed. The life of someone she'd been with was gone, and the person who'd done it was right in front of her.

"Look, Mikey, I'm about to get high, so can you just watch the door for me?"

I was not in the right state of mind to tell her how fucking stupid that was with the cops still possibly outside, but all I could do was nod and watch her do it. The way she did it was practiced. She had it down perfectly. When she pressed the needle in, she let out a gasp of air and relaxed against the bedframe.

"You should mess up your hair more. Your look right now is much better than your sweater hair."

Again, I just nodded. Her words didn't affect me. All I could think of were my actions. Actions always had consequences, and now I had to evade facing them. I looked over to Lily, who was staring at me, and scooted closer. I put my face close to hers so I could see her blue eyes and kissed her. I held this for what seemed like forever before pulling away to see her reaction. "You really are," she began to smile and laugh before putting her head down on her pillow. I again could not find words for why I'd just done that. All I knew was that it had made me feel better. Better than any stupid benzo could.

"I know you won't talk. You never do. So just," she motioned her arms in a circle, "stay here with me for now."

With that, she'd promptly passed out in the next ten minutes. I felt tired from what my body had endured and curled up at the other end of her bed and closed my eyes. I'd felt on top of the world today. Now all I felt was under the world, burning in hell. Every day was supposed to be great from now on, with school done and money coming in. But reality had set in. The day would come when I wasn't.

Endings and Beginnings

Today was a new day, a new week, and a new beginning. I was finishing my second-to-last week of school and would be able to focus on the emptiness in my life once summer came. Since I'd finally be of age to move out or do whatever I wanted, the possibility of all that was enticing.

This week I was on a mission. I'd visited Katrina and cleaned up loose ends there. I'd left in the morning, and she was surprised to see me but couldn't help but cry.

"My baby is finally home."

That was all she said to me. "Yes, she is," I'd said while putting on my shoes and leaving. If only Katrina had known that was all my handiwork. I had saved her.

It seemed nothing was stopping me in life now except for the random police officer and the strange issue with Trey about laying low, but I suspected that would only be for a short time. Right now, I had a date to look forward to.

Nicole had been talking to me all week, but she knew nothing about Lily. She kept wanting to take me to a spot out of town and get food, which I agreed to. With Nicole, I didn't have to talk too much. She understood me on a deeper level. I'd realized that the night she came and picked me up with no hesitation. This whole week, I'd caught myself staring at her in class or looking at her when I passed her in the hallway.

The concept of love had always eluded me. I'd always loved Lily. Maybe I'd had the idea wrong the whole time, though. I'd wanted to "save" Lily, but I'd never felt profound affection for her except on some rare occasions in the past. I was starting to understand that it's not a one-way road. It's a freeway and can mean a multitude of things. I knew that when Nicole kissed me, I felt a deep, romantic love. When Lily and I kissed, I'd done it at my lowest point. I felt something, but had no clue what it was.

Coming back to the present world, I was sitting in my living room, staring at the phone screen. It displayed the time and two birds that would fly off the tiny screen every ten seconds. Glancing to my left, my mother was up and about. She was enjoying the sun and sitting outside in our backyard. It made me happy to know she could experience some happiness. One day, I hoped she'd be back to her regular self in some way. It was up to me and how hard I worked. Not just the money, but also by being a good son. Maybe in the future, I could even have a child, which I bet she'd adore.

My daydreaming came to an end as the birds flew off and I received a text from Nicole: here :P. I put my phone away, stood up, and took another look at my mother. She seemed to be in a state of zen I didn't want to disturb. I went to the table and wrote a quick note. I'm going out with my friend Nicole, and I'll be back later. Love you, Mom. Seeing as this was good enough, I went outside, locked the door, and headed over to Nicole's car. She drove a beautiful all-black 1997 Camry XLE that reminded me of my father's car, as he'd always driven Toyotas.

Going over and seeing her in the driver's seat, I couldn't help but smile, which she returned. I opened the door and slid in. The radio was on, this time playing pop instead of the classics she usually did.

"Switching it up?" I asked with a laughing side-eye.

"It's just one of those days where I want to drive fast and listen to current artists," she replied, twirling her brunette hair.

I lifted my eyebrow. "Drive fast?"

She blushed at this and told me to shut up, laughing.

"We have all day, so where do you want to go first, sir?" Nicole made a mocking gesture, as if she were a taxi driver.

"This day is yours to plan, so just surprise me. We can do anything," I said. Truth be told, I'd never hung out with people who had access to a car, so I wanted to go anywhere so we could see and do everything.

Putting the car into drive, we started out of town. I glanced at her and asked for a clue as to where we'd be going first. All she gave me was "West."

As we drove out of town, I loved seeing all the green in the trees illuminated by the sun. Everything looked beautiful, and I felt at peace. Nicole knew I didn't like to talk, which was such a relief. We'd glance over at each other and smile while listening to the latest pop song. I'd forgotten the feeling of being with someone who understood you.

"You know, Mikey, I have my own secrets. Why I want to leave this place. Why I fell in love with you."

I responded with a smile. "Your secret is safe with me."

Nicole played with her hair as she spoke. "I had dreams that I would leave this small town. Go to a big city. But I'd go with a guy from my small town. Just him

and me. Leaving together. Inseparable. I never imagined
you would be the one, and it's just all so surreal to me."

I gave a laugh. "Would you want it to be someone
else?"

She shook her head. "No, that's not what I mean. I'm
glad I have you. It's just, my parents have so many
expectations for me, my friends are always talking about
how we're all going to go to college together and be
roommates. It's overwhelming."

I understood what she meant in every way. If I'd had
any friends, that is. "Well, I'm happy to be by your side."

She bit her nail. "Michael, don't get mad at me, but
how do I know that you, you know, won't leave me too?
This whole town is fake to me, and it feels like I always
get the short end of the stick."

My throat tightened hearing her say this. "I won't let
that happen. I am a man of my word. I can make things
happen. We'll go to that big city. If I'm with you, I can do
anything."

She leaned over and kissed me. "Forever."

"Forever."

After a while of comfortable silence, she brought up
something else. "Do you see that Cadillac behind us?"

I nodded yes.

"I swear, I don't know if I'm imagining it, but it's been
behind me since I left."

"It's weird, but it's probably just on the same path," I
told her.

Other than that, we were arriving at a random diner
with neon lights called Lenna's.

I do notice things, and I like to believe it's my best
quality, so I took it to heart and looked for the car when
we got out, but didn't see it drive by. I thought about
telling Nicole, but didn't want to worry her, as she
seemed in such an excellent mood. Walking inside and

sitting down at the booth, I looked at her and realized just how wonderful she looked.

It was as if my whole perspective of her had changed, and I felt compelled to look away. I told her I had to wash my hands before I ate and headed to the restroom. Once in there, I washed my hands, slapped some cold water on my face, and took a Xanax from my wallet. The bitter taste without water almost made me gag, but it made me realize I couldn't remember the last time I'd taken one today.

Maybe it was a sign that being focused on something new and exciting takes away your need for substances. I'd think about that later and left the restroom. Luckily, the waitress arrived just as we were ready to order, and I got my usual Coke with a corn dog and fries.

"Can never go wrong with those three," I told Nicole, trying to be conversational. She'd gotten the same, but no corn dog. The taste of the alprazolam in my mouth was killing me, and I had to wait ages for our food and drinks. The food was surprisingly good, but I'd gotten the most basic stuff, so I shouldn't have been that surprised.

Nicole kept talking to me about how her last week at school went and how she needed to decide where to go to college.

"Oh? College. I haven't even really thought about that," I muttered off to the side. I had no ambitions for college and wanted school to be permanently done by the end of next week. Going for over fifteen years, then paying for four more years was not my forte. She sipped her Coke. "I might have to move out of state to where the colleges are. I applied for about seven of them."

A sharp pain stung my heart. I hadn't realized the possibility that she could be leaving.

"Hopefully, you can take me along with you," I replied in a sad and joking tone. I wasn't sure which one came across to her.

"I can help you figure out what you want to do and how to apply, if you want," Nicole said, smiling and reaching out to touch my hand. I nodded and thought it over. I could do that to spend time with her, but I wouldn't be going to further education. My mind was made up. I wondered who else might leave me. Not Lily? I couldn't be thinking of her right now.

Finishing my drink, I went up to pay. Nicole pulled out her wallet, but I told her I had it and paid with a twenty, told them to keep the change as a tip. Walking back out and holding the door open for her felt strange. I didn't want her to go just when I felt like I had everything under control.

Looking up at the stars, Nicole grabbed my hand and thanked me. "That was a very gentlemanly move, Mikey."

I told her it was no problem and I'd enjoyed the food more than I thought I would. I asked her where we were going next. She turned on the car as I was hopping in. "Well, it's getting dark, so we can go to the place I've been wanting to take you to."

As she was saying this, I swore I saw a Cadillac drive down the road. Maybe I was being paranoid, but if it were a cop or someone tailing me, they'd know I was a perfect person doing perfectly normal things. Still, it sent a shiver down my spine. I refocused and told her I was excited to go to the next place. After that, we could go to my house and watch a movie.

If my mother were up, this plan would come crashing down harder than my stomach when meeting that officer, but who knew with her nowadays. Maybe she'd be happy to have someone else in the house for a change. I knew it must get lonely being in there all day, which is why I was glad to see her out and not drinking. Things were turning around for her, which made me happy, and if she was up, I could even introduce Nicole. I felt like they'd get along perfectly.

Down the road, we drove past endless trees while the sky darkened. All you could see were the yellow signs the headlights would hit, the stars in front of you, and the forest of trees that went on forever. She kept changing radio stations until she found one playing classics, which I thought was more like her. "We're almost there," she said, looking at me in a cute voice.

I did wonder where she was taking me, especially since it was so dark. It was probably dangerous to be out in the middle of nowhere because of animals, car issues, and, God forbid, a human. My father had always told me the scariest thing in the forest is not an animal. It's a human. I had no clue how to fix car issues, but I had complete trust in her. However, I felt naked with no weapon on me this far out. I couldn't fight for shit. I just always told myself I could use my brain to win against someone else. I hated overthinking. I was here with a beautiful girl, and I was having stupid anxiety about how dark it was, like a little kid. "We're here," she told me as we pulled off onto a side dirt road. The car drove for about half a mile, and then she parked.

"This is going to blow your mind. Trust me, the first time I saw it, I wished I could stay here forever."

She looked so excited. This must be an essential place for her, and based on her reaction, I felt a little honored. Following her lead, she did a twirl and motioned for me to follow.

We walked down a small trail, and I couldn't help but wonder how the hell she knew this place in the darkness. As we walked, she whistled for a while, something I could never do. I told her I was jealous she could do that, to which she said with a smile, "I'll help you learn in the future."

I let her know I'd be happy to learn and then pulled out my phone, which showed the time as 11:57. No signal.

We came out of the clearing, and my mind was blown. Ever since I'd started pills, I'd become a robot. Nothing was interesting or beautiful to me in any way. This, however, looking at Nicole and the clearing we were in, gave me a grasp on older memories of how life can be beautiful when it's not dull. I'd always loved bodies of water and loved water in general, whether it was snow, rain, whatever.

For a brief moment, I took in all my surroundings, feeling pure bliss. The darkness surrounded me, but the beauty clarified my vision, and my mind delved into so many thoughts. The drive here, my childhood, my father, my drugs, sunsets, and everything else. I was snapped out of it as I heard Nicole yell out to me. "Look!"

There was a waterfall that led into the lake I was looking at, and she was tying her hair up to go into it. It wouldn't drench you. It was more like a trickle you'd see at a cave entrance. She held out her hand to it and watched. I wondered what she was doing.

She motioned for me to come over with a slight wave of her right hand, so I got up and walked over.

"Okay, look, when I'm here I always put my palm out and watch the water go off all my fingers," Nicole told me happily. I asked her why that made her so happy.

"Well, it's like all of life in a way. Your fingers catch the water, and it goes in all different directions, purely based on the choices of the life around us. It's beautiful."

I wanted to point out that finger size and the angle you were positioned at probably played a part too, but I ignored that and stuck out my hand.

My hand felt the cold water as I spread my fingers and watched it go in lines and fall, creating its own waterfall. A waterfall designed by human intervention. What a fascinating thing. I walked towards the back to sit down where Nicole was. I noticed her hair was wet and her shirt was still off.

"It's like my own mini hideout. Nobody would be able to find me here at night," she said in a slightly sad voice. "You wouldn't even believe how I found this place in the first place."

She looked at me. I shrugged.

"I was pissed at my parents and decided to drive until I had half a tank and just walk into the woods. I got halfway through and was about to stop on the side of the road in dirt when I saw a tiny path, and here we are today."

I looked at her. "Yeah, that is some incredible luck. I would kill to have a place like this where I could go to be alone."

She laughed. "Well, don't get any ideas. I don't want to die before my graduation."

I shook my head with a smile. "I love that you took me here. It's beautiful. I want to come back and swim in the lake, and I have to show you how I skip stones."

I don't know why I brought that up, as I'd stopped talking about it when my father died since it reminded me of him. Fortunately, she thought the idea would be great and said she'd be able to skip over the whole lake. She got up, wrapped her shirt and sweater around her stomach, and came over. "Is it okay if I rest on you?"

I nodded. She lay on me, half naked, and I didn't know what to do. This was such a beautiful sight: a waterfall entrance in front of me, a beautiful girl lying on me, darkness, and stars in the night sky.

I didn't say a word until I heard her start to talk, her jaw moving against my leg.

"Aren't you going to ask me?"

My heart thumped at this statement. Did she mean to ask her out? I'd never had a girlfriend, and I doubted I'd be good at it.

"Ask you to be my girlfriend?" I said in a cautious tone.

She started to laugh and poked at my feet. "Duh."

Time seemed to feel like forever in that moment. Did I want her to be my girlfriend? Would I have to tell her everything I did? Would she like the real me? What if she left for college? I had too many questions, but my hormones bested me.

"Nicole, would you be my girlfriend?"

She squeezed my hand and got up to kiss me. I took this as a definitive yes.

We held hands for a while and watched the waterfall. My hands started to shake in a way, so I told her, "Nicole, you're the first person I've ever dated. Like a real relationship."

She looked at me funny. "Well, the same goes for me."

My eyes must have given me away because she said, "Surprised? I was never interested in the people around me. I liked how you didn't try to fit in. I liked how you stand out, and you're confident."

I shook my head. "I'm nothing like that. Where did you get that from?"

Nicole waved me off. "The first day we did the journal readings, you volunteered to go first and talk about your dreams and weren't nervous in the slightest."

I didn't know that people noticed me, so this was new. That couldn't be all, though.

"Just from the journal readings?" I asked, interested.

She twirled her hair. "Well, after that, I would watch you sometimes at school and see what you did. You just stood out to me. I was so happy when you agreed to go to the party because I thought, with the way you acted, that wasn't something you'd do."

Well, I'd had other plans for that night, which was the only reason I went, but I had to admit I was shocked that another human had taken an interest in me. Surely she knew about Lily, then. That was the only person I'd be at school with and care about. I didn't want to bring that up unless she did.

"Nobody had ever asked me to do anything like that, so I thought, why not? And it was a cute girl asking me, so how could I say no?"

I told her as she giggled. After that, she lay into me and fell asleep softly. I could hear her tiny little snores. An actual human was lying on me, and she was beautiful, and I was the only one here with her. She trusted me with her life. What a strange feeling.

After an hour of lying in the cave entrance, I took off my sweater, bundled it up, and lay my head on it.

"I'll be back, Nicole," I whispered to her. Walking out of the cave, I felt the wonderful air mixed with the water. The lake in front of me was so calm, and I told myself I was going to get twenty skips after I went to the car and got my wallet. I had to re-up on my Xanax, and it had been a couple of hours. Lucky me to be addicted to the drug with the worst half-life.

Stupidly, I'd left it in her car, which wasn't like me. None of this was like me, but after how amazing tonight was, I wasn't one to complain. Her keys had been on a rock next to her phone, so I just needed to navigate back to the car, which I was pretty sure was close. There was no key fob, and even if there was, I didn't want to use it in the middle of the night.

The forest around me sounded dead quiet, which was starting to freak me out. I knew I had to get my Xanax if I was getting scared this easily. A peaceful forest was always a bad sign, as my father had told me. I remembered telling him at a young age that I didn't want to go deep into the forest because of the animals.

"As long as you can hear the noises around you, you are safe."

Looking back, that advice seemed questionable, but I guess that's what you have to do to reassure your son.

Finally, I spotted her car and ran over to it. It was so quiet, every move I made echoed for eternity, it seemed. Putting the key in the car lock, it didn't work. God, I must be tired. I tried again with no luck. I didn't understand. These were the car keys, I thought as I looked down at them. Maybe they unlocked the trunk? I went to the back and tried, but couldn't find the lock. Was I this fucked up from going a couple of hours without pills?

I thought if I pulled out my phone to use as a flashlight, I could get it open. My heart was racing, and I felt a panic attack coming on. My mind flashed to Nicole waking up alone, Nicole being taken, and my mind began to spiral. Focus. I got out my phone light and found the trunk lock. I stared in horror as I brought my phone up to it and read the word Cadillac.

My mind freaked out as I looked all around me like a madman. The fucking car that had been following us. What did I do now? I needed to be calm and couldn't find the Camry. I decided Nicole was more important and made a mad dash through the forest. It was still quiet, which I couldn't understand. This was a human out here. Why would the woods be quiet?

When I came out of the forest, I was on the other side. I started to run over when my heart dropped and went up again. Staring at me was a boy my age whom I knew. This was Thomas's friend, Connor. All I could think was that I needed a Xanax, as just seeing him had almost killed me. I needed to get to Nicole. The person in front of me did not matter in my realm of existence.

"You look like you've seen a ghost, Michael. Maybe you have." the entity said in a wicked manner.

To me, he was no longer human. All I needed to do was make sure Nicole was okay. I moved to the right to try to sidestep him, but I was pushed back. Looking at me demonically, he spat at my feet. "Do you think I'm going to let you go that easily?"

He started to laugh as I stared at him blankly. I twisted my right hand in question. "What do you want, and why are you here?"

Connor didn't move while he talked. He stood there, staring daggers into my body. "I followed you out here. I didn't know you had a car. Pretty nice for someone coming from a poor, broken family." He started to mock, with fake tears for me. Did this mean he didn't know Nicole was here? He'd only been behind us and had never seen me with anyone besides Lily occasionally, who he knew wouldn't be here. I had to find out what he knew.

"Why have you been in the woods stalking me and following me while I drove out here?" I asked in a fake scared voice.

Connor finally moved, picking up a rock from the ground and tossing it up and down in his hand. "The police wouldn't do anything to you, even though I knew it was you." He yelled the last part, and I felt his emotion, which surprised me.

"I couldn't believe my eyes when I saw you running through the forest like a maniac. I popped your tire and was waiting for you to come back tired from whatever the fuck you were doing and beat the shit out of you. Imagine my surprise when you started running all over the forest to where my car was."

He sounded insane, like a serial killer playing with his victim. Growing up, though, I'd taught myself the best way to get out of situations was to deny and never stop.

"Connor, I have no clue what you're talking about, and this is fucking creepy, man," I said as if it were the truth.

This only made him angrier. He walked over and reached out with his right hand to grab my neck. In that moment, I knew I wouldn't beat him in a fight, and my anxiety was killing me. It felt like death would be a preferable alternative to whatever my body was feeling. He started to choke me. "I know you hurt Thomas. Admit it, and I'll spare you."

It was getting harder to breathe by the second, and I didn't doubt he was serious. I tried to get some words out, but he let me go, and I dropped onto my back.

"Last chance, Mikey. I want to hear you say it."

I stood up, feeling a rush of adrenaline that felt like heroin but in a much better sense. I smiled crookedly at him. "Thomas? The worthless drug dealer who wanted to rape Lily? Yeah, that Thomas? I stabbed him." His eyes were enraged as I said this.

"Do you want to know how I stabbed him?" Connor looked at me with rage but didn't move. "I'll show you how I did it."

I immediately dove towards Connor's knees to knock him off balance. He stumbled back and got up. I felt so much energy that I knew I could take him. I would make him hurt and let him go.

We stood at an impasse, looking at each other. The sounds around us were dead quiet. The lake sparkled in the moonlight and stars above. I wished I didn't have to do this. Connor ran at me, trying to grab my right hand, which I was blocking with, and I pulled back and grabbed the back of his shirt. On the ground, I punched him over and over. He put his hands up, but it made no difference. My hands felt so raw that I finally let him go.

He rolled over, crying and moaning in pain as I got up to tell him to let this issue go. Instead, he looked at me. "You know what Thomas wanted to do to Lily? He should have. You couldn't have stopped him."

My face didn't change as he said these words. Only my motive did. I grabbed the back of his shirt and pushed his face above the lake. I wanted to ask if he had any last words, but decided it would be better to determine if he understood what was about to happen. All he did was let out a pitiful cry, which annoyed me, and I put his head into the water.

Either he was stronger than I thought, or my adrenaline had worn off. With his arms, he was able to drag me into the water with him. The dark water surrounding me was murky. All I knew was that I had to concentrate on him. I reached out for his neck and caught hold of it. I didn't know how long I could hold my breath, but I was going down with this ship.

We tossed and turned as he jabbed his legs and arms at me. At one point, I almost lost control as he poked me in the eye so hard my reflexes nearly made my hands divert from his neck to my eye. My anxiety was making it harder to breathe, and I felt as if I would die in this murky darkness. He struggled for a while, God knows how long, until it was over. I waited five more seconds before pushing to the surface to get air.

I had to make sure I had everything on me: car keys, phone, wallet. I sat on the edge of the lake, gasping for air. I needed a Xanax, and now I knew the car was on the other side. I pushed and limped my way over to where it should be, and it was there. Thank you, Connor. I took four of them without water and locked the car. Limping back, I could feel my body regulate and a sense of euphoria take over.

I heard the crack of a branch and immediately knew what was there.

"You didn't even check if I was dead, you stupid fuck."

Connor said this as he dove at me. I was in too much pain to even move, so I took the hit and let him do his worst, but all he could muster was a few punches before falling over. I turned on my side, watching him crawl towards his car, looking like a wet dog.

I decided I needed to make peace with him, or this bullshit would never end. I called out. "Connor, let's call it even. There's no need for this anymore."

Connor was wounded, and not just physically. He could barely breathe as he reached his car. I heard his ragged breath over and over in the quiet of the forest. "You're not worth my time, Michael," he said, swinging himself up into his car.

I didn't understand him. Maybe the shock of us both almost drowning had changed his mind on his vengeful pursuit of me. I didn't even know what I'd done wrong to him other than hurt his friend. Like he said, though, I wasn't worth his time, and neither was he. I needed to focus on what was happening here as I watched Connor drive off.

I decided to process all this and catch my breath. I watched the lake and the reflection of the sky. Nothing had happened here. I was watching the lake, trying to get it to go back to its beautiful form.

I walked back as slowly as possible to the waterfall entrance. I felt the lake's murkiness on me as I stumbled, and my mind made me shudder. I had tried to kill another human being, and it was all over me. I was going to hell for what I'd done. There was no reason for me to have done that. Finally reaching the entrance, I stood in front of it and stepped into the waterfall as I let it wash away all my sins.

I stepped out of the waterfall and found myself walking back towards the lake. I didn't know why. Flashes of being in that murky water flooded through my brain. Coughing up water as I dragged myself out. I walked over to the edge where it happened and stared at it.

The lake had returned to its original form, like nobody had ever been inside. My heart hurt so bad as my mind circled around the thoughts of drowning. One of us could have drowned. It was so close to being me. I collapsed near it with my hand hanging into the water and stared at the stars.

Every star I stared at was dead. By the time we would ever reach one, it would be dead. My whole body trembled as I thought of this. Was it too late for me? Was Nicole the redeeming factor, or was she traveling towards a star that was already dead?

Getting up, my legs wobbled and I fell down again. I let go of all the muscles in my body and collapsed to cry. I had nothing left to cry for. I just wanted to never feel that sensation again. Being dragged down, coughing up water, and now the water dripped over my face as if to mock me. I had no strength left. I was truly alone. A dead fucking star.

Numb

The pain I felt staring at myself was excruciating. No amount of drugs could fix what I'd done. I was a wicked person, a monster, and I'd done it all to myself. Yet I was destined to keep going. If I had to be a terrible person, I'd make the best of it and keep moving forward. Forward and only forward was the only option for me.

After taking my pills the night before, Nicole had dragged me to the car and somehow fixed the tire. She'd recounted to me that I was talking nonsense and had insisted I lie in the back. I knew I was in trouble with her, and I hated myself for it. The one good person in this world most likely hated me now. Either she thought I was drunk, or who knows what. All I could remember was that she dropped me off, and now I was here.

The only benefit I'd give to these godforsaken pills was that there was no hangover, so I was able to get to work immediately. I sent in an order on the darknet for a thousand alprazolam, which Trey would buy for four grand. Getting in the orders was always a pain: transferring money to online currency, waiting hours, then triple-checking my order was correct. All it did was give me time to reflect on what had gone on.

I sat at the edge of my bed. I held up my hands and watched them shake. I tried my best to stop them, commanding my brain to relax. All they did was shake as if I were still choking Connor in that awful water. I didn't want to remember any of that. I had failed in so many ways, and was sure to be caught soon. Failure. Failure. I was a failure. My brain was right. I couldn't control my emotions and had nearly killed another person, this time doing it directly.

Sitting there, I wondered about ending it all. Getting out of this world. It would be like a Monopoly card, a get-out-of-jail-free card. No consequences for my actions. Like father, like son. No. I would never do what he did. I would continue forward. Each day, step by step. I would make amends with Nicole, help my mother and Lily, graduate, and stay ahead of the police.

Hearing this in my head, I got the motivation to accept that I would finish out my last week of school. All I had to do was beat that, and I was done. Today was Sunday, which meant I had hours to kill, so I decided to walk to the store to get some cigarettes and a Coke.

Leaving my house, I walked forward along the empty roads of my small town. The sky was a cloudy gray, and I saw a flock of birds flying towards the forest. If they could be free, so could I. Everything around me seemed more gray than usual. The color was sucked out of my life. I walked down the road, kicking rocks and looking for any signs of life.

When I arrived at the gas station, the clerk wasn't there, which was slightly annoying. I walked around and got my Coke. The color red was so bright on it. A color I never wanted to see again. I put it back and got a Pepsi instead. The blue reminded me of rain and water, which I liked. Going back to the counter, the clerk had appeared somehow and was eyeing me. "Switching up sodas?"

I pulled out my wallet. "Sometimes you just need a change. Two packs of Lucky Strikes and a lighter, please."

After I got out, I lit up a Lucky and decided to go in a random direction. Truly, there were only three, because I didn't want to go home. Inhaling the nicotine as hard as I could made me feel dizzy, which made me feel a bit better because I was feeling something. I'd been worried that I was becoming something evil, something with no emotions. I didn't know if this counted, but it was a start.

In the back of my mind, I realized my brain had picked where to walk on purpose. I was walking towards the school and was a block away. Inhaling and exhaling, I threw away the cigarette when I got to the gate and climbed it. Why was I going here? My mind was on autopilot and wouldn't let me stop.

Finally, I ended up at the dugout. The dugout where I'd watched Lucas overdose and choke on his own vomit. A boy whose eyes watched mine the whole time. A boy who was conscious of what kind of person I truly was, even if it was just for fifteen minutes. Sitting on the bench, I lit up another Lucky and started to chain-smoke. I put my left hand to my face and stared at the ground. My future wasn't looking bright with all the things I'd done, not to mention the fact that Trey could get rid of me at any time, and Nicole or Lily could leave.

Who would I live for then? I could convince myself I was doing it for my mom, but eventually I wouldn't be able to stand it. My life shouldn't have to consist of work forever, which is why I was so damn jealous of those birds I'd seen earlier. The freedom to travel the earth and not have any human responsibilities.

I lay on my back and lit up another Strike. I wondered if my mom would come to my graduation. It hurt to think my dad wouldn't be coming. It wasn't an accomplishment or anything huge. I just wanted my family there, as silly as it sounds. God, I felt so pathetic. At least my brain wasn't calling me a failure yet. Looking around, I got chills and decided to leave, as something felt off.

The closest place was Lily's, which was halfway between school and my house. I should have been going to Nicole's since we were dating now, but I remembered the kiss Lily had given me. Plus, I was a friend of their family and had helped Katrina. I felt excited at the prospect of seeing her. It had become a rare occurrence, unlike how it used to be, which made it feel so much different.

Passing through the street with the cloudy sky over me, I wondered what was in store. Was she going through withdrawals or still using? Was she grieving the loss of her boyfriend or the trauma she'd been through? Asking myself these questions made me realize I was directly responsible for everything I'd just asked. I'd gotten her hooked on drugs. I'd killed her boyfriend. I'd given her lifelong trauma.

I sat down on the nearest porch, thinking this over. I was only trying to help her, but I'd ruined her life way before. Deep in thought, a strange occurrence happened: a black cat in the yard was staring at me. I'd always loved seeing wild cats and trying to get them to come to me, but for some reason, I knew this one had no intention. It stared at me with its yellow eyes before I finally turned away to look back down the steps. Sneaking a glance at it again showed it was still staring at me.

Even for a cat, I realized how truly terrifying it is to stare at someone and never break their gaze. I decided to go over and try to pet it, expecting it to run away, but it let me touch it. The cat didn't purr. It just turned its head around to stare at me, and then into the heavens. I felt so numb to all this that I dismissed it as a regular occurrence and left.

Coming up to her house, I didn't know what I was going there for. What would I say to her? What condition would she be in? My wrecked mind kept remembering that kiss she'd given me, over and over, making it impossible to think. I had so much going on in my head, I felt as if it was going to explode if I told someone. Make it stop, I kept repeating to myself as I knocked on her door.

"Michael!"

I hadn't had a second to think before I looked up and saw her mom with a huge smile.

"I'm so glad you stopped by. Lily has been home now for a while, and I think it'd be great if she saw you. Do you want something to drink?"

I shook my head no. "Thank you, though, and I'm glad to hear she's been home. I'm hoping we can finish off the school year strong."

I didn't even know what that sentence meant. My mind was obliterated, and it was choosing to speak like a robot.

"Yes, I think the graduation will be wonderful. Lily has told me she hasn't been planning on going to prom, and I don't blame her for what she went through." Katrina looked sad as she said this. "I just hope she can take the time she needs to recover."

Prom? I'd forgotten that even existed. I guessed that's what happens when you don't talk to anyone.

"She'll get through it. I know her too well," I said boldly. Katrina gave me a half smile. I knew she could tell something was bugging me but didn't inquire.

"Well, Lily's upstairs. I'll be down here if you two need anything," Katrina said as she got up from the table. I thanked her and walked up to her room. I gave two light knocks, to which she replied, "I already know who it is."

Taking this as a yes to come in, I opened the door and saw Lily sitting on the ground, staring at her mirror, doing something with her hair.

"How did you know it was me?" I was too confused to come up with a solution. She stared at the mirror. "What other person is going to come visit the dead junkie's girlfriend?"

This caught me off guard. "I feel like they'd be more inclined to visit you because of that reason, Lil."

She shook her head at me. "People at school think I made him overdose, and I was using him for drugs constantly up to the point where he died. Drugwhore, I heard them calling me. I guess we're both killers now."

My head throbbed violently at that comment as I sat down and wished I'd asked Katrina for water. My heart was beating so fast, I pulled out my wallet and took some Xanax to calm it down. Lily held out her blonde hair to inspect it, then looked at me through the mirror. "You always take those stupid pills that do nothing. Why don't you take one that will make you feel good for once?"

With this, she got up, went to her drawer, grabbed some pills, and came over to me. "These are Vicodin. Use them when you feel down, and you'll feel in the right state of mind."

I wasn't in any state of mind right now. I felt worse and worse. I took the pills because any promise of feeling better, on even a one percent chance it might work, would save my life. Lily put the rest in my pocket and stood up. "Hold onto those. Also, can you tell me if my hair is blonde or if it's turning brunette?"

I looked her over to see why the fuck we were talking about this and told her it was blonde.

"I knew it. Still blonde. Still the best."

Not knowing what to do or caring, I walked over to her bed, lay down in it, and stared at the wall. "Mikey, you can't just fucking sleep in..." She stopped midsentence. I had tears in my eyes, and my mental capacity was breaking down with every single thought. The madness I'd caused was consuming my soul, and there was nothing I could do about it except let it happen.

Crying overcame me as I couldn't hold it in any longer. I tried to think about happy memories like they teach you in primary school, but all I saw was my dead dad and my drunken mother.

"I hate myself. I'm the worst of the worst. I try to act like I'm this great guy who can go around fixing things all by himself, but in the end, I fail. I've done nothing in my life to have a happy thought. I'm a failure, and the worst one. The one that knows he's a failure and continues to be one."

"I'm here for you," someone said as light hands brushed through my hair. I closed my eyes as hard as I could. "No one is here for me. I've done nothing to earn your respect as a friend. I hurt you in the past, and I can't fix anything about it. I've done so many more terrible things that I can't talk to anyone about. They eat at my soul, leaving me lifeless like this. What you're looking at now is the result of a broken man, if I can even call myself that."

I felt her get into bed and start to hold me. I didn't deserve to be here with her after what I'd put her through. "No, you're wrong. I have always admired the way you go about your life. You're strong, and I've seen it. You started to sell drugs when I recommended it and kept doing it, but I was too scared to keep going after Thomas got hurt. You're not afraid to be alone at school, and you end up doing good things for good people. My mom couldn't stop talking about you the other day, about how you came over when I was gone. Mikey, you're suffering. You have to let your thoughts out. I know there's a good person in there, and I don't want to die without ever knowing him."

I felt obligated to turn around and answer her after she'd spoken to me in such a delicate manner. I looked into her beautiful eyes with tears of my own, creating an ocean between us through my vision.

"It's always been."

I stopped for a moment. I didn't know what was coming over me.

"It's always been you."

She looked back at me and responded, not missing a beat. "Only someone who loves themselves can love others."

Her words stung so badly that I wanted to drift off to another place.

"I can't do that, Lily."

Before letting her speak, I rolled over and got up. I didn't want to cry in front of her anymore. I walked to her door as she stood there, not speaking.

"Thanks for the advice and listening to me, Lil."

I wanted her to tell me to stop so badly as I headed into the hallway.

"I know the day will come when you will, Mikey."

I stopped and looked back at her and nodded. I walked down the stairs and didn't see Katrina, which I took to mean I was letting myself out.

The clouds in the sky had turned to light rain. I could cry now as tears formed in my eyes. The pills she'd given me had made me say all of that, I decided. There was no way my body could have uttered that on its own. Only someone who loves themselves can love others. How could I love myself? Everything I did made me hate myself even more. I walked back to the house in the rain, watching the birds fly around me. Not wanting to go in yet, I sat on the sidewalk while the rain piled down on me and lit up a Lucky.

Taking long drags from it, I got out my phone and called Nicole.

"Mikey?"

I switched my smoking position with my fingers. "Yeah, it's me. I just wanted to call and ask you about something."

She responded with sarcasm. "You know it's rude to call a girl and keep her waiting on a question, Mikey."

Taking a drag before answering, I exhaled as long as I could and let it out. I dropped the cigarette and watched the rain douse it.

"Do you want to go to prom with me?"

Apathy

The last week of school had been a bore. Everyone in my classes would huddle together, as finals were already done, and talk about which college they were applying to.

"I can't wait to get out of this town."

I heard this over and over, which made me wonder if I was insane for wanting to stay. I'd had my worst memories here, but it was my hometown, and I didn't want any changes in my life. The fewer people in town, the better, I thought.

During the week, I went to a clothing store to buy clothes for prom. Nicole had been elated that I'd wanted to go with her. "I was waiting for you to ask, but I thought you wouldn't because it's not your type of thing."

I hadn't been able to see her, but in my dreams at night, I always dreamt of a girl who looked like her. She truly was beautiful, and I had no clue what she saw in me, which I guessed should make me feel lucky, but I still felt bad. I'd almost killed a boy at her secret spot, no more than forty feet from her sleeping body. It felt ugly and cruel to think about.

To get through all this, I'd been taking the pills Lily had given me, as they did improve my mood. I'd stopped by her house to buy more and now carried them with me. I didn't have to take them throughout the day like Xanax, but being addicted to benzos, painkillers, and nicotine was not going to lead me down a good path. It was just for this week, I'd decided.

Other than that, I'd seen missing posters about Connor around town. I hadn't seen any police presence, which meant they weren't investigating it as a homicide, I assumed. This eased my worries a bit, but he was bound to show up sooner or later, and I needed to be prepared. I'd been with Nicole that whole night, and the alibi was solid except for the time frame when she was asleep. I didn't know how that would go over in an interrogation, but I didn't want to find out.

Walking home on Friday, I just wanted to go to bed and sleep. I'd felt exhausted and had been having heart palpitations. The whole time I was walking, I kept looking over my shoulder until I reached my front door. Going upstairs to my room, I looked out the window and was glad I'd gotten home in time, as I saw huge storm clouds approaching. Wanting to go to bed, I took a pill from my wallet and stared at the ceiling.

Minutes passed, until I wondered why I hadn't fallen asleep. Was my tolerance too high? I went over, wiping sweat from my forehead, to check my wallet. I opened the slot where I kept them and saw all my Xanax and barely any Vicodin. Immediately realizing my mistake, I took a Xanax as quickly as I could, thinking I could take one and then another in ten minutes.

I hit the floor and watched my wallet drop as my pills fell out.

"Why are you back here?"

I looked up to see Lily. I didn't have time to deal with her, so I punched her in the arm. "Leave me alone. I need to work on loving myself, remember?" I said, sneering at her. She laughed at me. "You'll never be able to love yourself, and I will never love you. You're a failure and a killer at heart. When something goes wrong, all you can do is think of the extremes. I could never love you."

I reached out to grab her before she disappeared.

Do you want to love yourself? No.

Do you love anyone? No.

What is your reason for existing? I didn't ask to exist.

No response?

Complete and utter failure.

The thunder shook my house so violently I had no idea if I was dead or dreaming. I saw my wallet with its contents fallen out, the last thing I'd seen before collapsing. My whole body ached as I tried to move. I was stuck in a fetal position and sore everywhere. Now my physical form was ruined too.

A lightning bolt flashed so bright next to my window. I sat there waiting for the explosion, hoping the next bolt would strike through the house and kill me. How could I have been so stupid to take the wrong pills today? Taking that Xanax right before I had the seizure probably saved my fucking life. I yearned for another one, but my body was too rigid to move.

Thunder exploded right next to my window, making my head burst open with new pain. In that moment, I saw everyone I'd hurt. The mangled mess I'd left rotted my brain while I put my hands to my head, begging for it to stop. The thunder only grew louder, and as it did, so did my guilt. "I need someone," I whimpered out desperately. Rolling over to grab my wallet, I took more Xanax and took out my phone and dialed the only person I could think of. I was so close to my bed that I put the phone on speaker, pulled a blanket hanging off my bed, and crawled under it.

The phone rang as the raindrops pelted my window. I hugged my blanket as if it were a heavenly object keeping me alive and centered in the world. I heard her say, "Mikey?"

Facing the phone, I tried my best to get words out. "Nicole, I. I can't take this anymore. I'm in so much pain."

She didn't respond for a few seconds, and I thought she'd hung up when she replied, "Are you home?"

I told her yes.

"I'm going to come over, okay? It's probably just the storm, and we can sit through it."

I didn't want her to drive through this hell I was hearing outside. I found my voice. "It's too dangerous, Nicole. I just wanted to talk to you."

This wasn't going to convince her, as I sounded like I was dying whenever I spoke. She told me she was coming and didn't care about the storm. "I've lived through a million of these."

When the phone line went dead, I lay there with my blanket, watching the shadows dance around my room as if the rain was mocking me. The shadows turned into people I'd hurt, then they turned into cops chasing me. Then it was two shadows: me sitting on the ground, and the other yelling at me, which was Lily. I was losing my mind from the drugs, from paranoia. I felt in that moment that a bullet to the head might be the nicest feeling in the world.

I lay there before realizing the phone line was still dead, emitting static. How much time had passed? I crawled out and stumbled downstairs, trying not to look at the reflecting shadows on all the walls. I assumed she'd call when she was here, so I waited. Minutes went by until I realized my phone was still upstairs, the line still dead and ringing. I couldn't go back up there. I knew Nicole would show up. She had to. Something had to go right for me.

I went to my door and opened it to watch for her. Feelings of uncertainty clouded my mind. Did she get into an accident? Had I killed another person? I had to find her, I thought, as my brain dragged my body into the thunderstorm outside.

"Nicole?"

I yelled. This was useless, as the wind was so loud that nobody could hear me within ten yards. I got out into the road when I saw a car with its hazards on, parked. I knew this had to be her and urged myself forward before my body gave out.

I fell hard in the water surrounding me, but luckily I'd put my arms out in time. My body had suffered too much from the seizure, and I was realizing I couldn't move. I hadn't even noticed the rain and how hard it was hitting me. Surely this was it for me. To die right outside my house in a thunderstorm with my body crippled. It was what I deserved.

I closed my eyes and let everything happen to me. I heard thunder so loud I thought the ground was breaking and saw lightning through my closed eyelids. God was cruel to me in this way. Could I not have a seizure now? I had to freeze to death in water with none of my body parts working. The thought of dying seemed so close, and I knew I was going to hell. If I was already going there, I wished I could have lived more of my life before being sentenced to eternal punishment. I am a failure.

I don't know how long I was stuck there until a car passed by me slowly, and my body was dragged into my house. I couldn't feel anything. No emotions, no physical pain. I just let everything that was happening happen. My clothes were taken off, and I was walking somewhere inside. I was laid into a tub where the water was turned on. The hot water brought life back into me, but I still couldn't move or understand anything. I was utterly broken.

The water around me encapsulated my soul as if I were drifting off to sleep. A towel was wrapped around me, and I lay back against the side of the tub.

"Everything's going to be okay, Michael," a worried voice said. I smiled at this but still couldn't talk or move. My body hated my brain.

After a while, my body was hoisted up with someone's arms under my armpits in a lock. It took them a couple of tries, but I was on my feet. The next thing I knew, I was being walked towards my bed and having covers put over me. I could still hear the thunder and rain, but it felt so far away, as if it were from a dream I was waking up from. My reality faded, and my body gave out after the damage I'd done to it.

Behavior

I awoke in a state of mind that perplexed me. I couldn't remember anything, nor could I remember my dream. I flexed my right hand to see that my body was working and turned around to see my window. As I turned, I felt cold and realized I had no clothes on, which was odd because I always slept with my boxers and shirt on. Sitting up in bed using my blanket to cover me, I almost had a heart attack as I saw another person in my room asleep against some blankets and clothing from my closet.

I soon realized this was Nicole and wondered how many benzos I'd taken that had left me unable to remember anything. Why in the world was she on the floor, and did I want to wake her up? I tried to remember, but the only thing that came to me was how sore my body was and that I was able to move it. I remembered not being able to move, which must have been a traumatic experience for the brain, I assumed.

Making as little noise as possible, I walked over to my drawer and put on some clothes. Putting my arms and legs into them hurt even worse than I remembered. I felt better knowing I wasn't naked anymore. I pulled on an oversized hoodie to hide my body and walked over to the bed and whispered, "Nicole?"

Her eyes snapped open wildly, scanning the room before centering on me. I watched as her face went from happy to sad in an instant. She walked over and held me as tight as she could.

My body ached, but the warm embrace of her kindness overpowered the pain that plagued my bones. She touched my cheek. "Please don't ever do that again."

I wanted to ask her what I'd done. I had no clue what had happened, and my mind was reeling with paranoia. I reached out to flex my right hand and gripped hers. "Can you tell me what happened?"

Nicole let out a long sigh and sat down next to me.

"I was in my car, a minute away from your house, when the water had overfilled a part of the street that I couldn't pass. I called you repeatedly while watching your house. Then I saw someone walk out, which I thought was odd because from your voice, it sounded like you were in pain. The rain was so strong that the next second you were gone, and I thought I was seeing things."

She grabbed both her hands together like she didn't want to keep talking.

"I decided to lock my car and go through the water to see if that was you. I barely made it over the running water and was cursing at myself for being such an idiot, but I knew you were in trouble. And then that's when I saw you. You were facing the sky on your back, drenched in water surrounding you like blood leaking from a dead body. I went over and screamed at you, but you didn't move or respond."

She stopped again and looked at me. "I messed up, and you could have died."

I looked at her and my hands, and as I flexed them again, I said, "I'm alive. You didn't mess up, Nicole."

She had tears in her eyes that glistened down her cheeks to her hair, which was oddly blonde to me.

"I went to get my phone out of my pocket and dial 911, but the rain was too strong and I kept pushing buttons until it fell away into a stream and was swept off. I thought I had killed you, Michael."

I didn't want to make her feel worse than she already did, as I could see she was in absolute agony.

"Hey, look at me. I'm here. I'm alive. You saved me. How'd you do it?"

She hesitated but responded. "I had no other option but to hope your door was unlocked. With that in mind, I dragged you to the house. It felt like you weighed a thousand pounds with all the water on your clothes. Luckily, the door was open, and I could see your house. I didn't know what to do, and I was panicking. I called out for anyone, but nobody responded. I knew your room was upstairs and could get you into other clothes to prevent hypothermia, so I helped you up the stairs. You made various noises and grunts, and I think you were conscious at some points. When we got upstairs, I looked down the hallway and saw your empty bedroom with the phone in front of it and blankets next to it."

I interrupted her as she paused. "It doesn't sound like you did anything wrong, Nicole. You saved my life. I can't remember a single thing."

She winced at my comment and looked down. "You can't?"

I shook my head no. She stared forward and pointed towards the bathroom. "As I was walking you towards your room, I saw the bathroom and decided the best thing to do was to get you heat. I undressed you and filled up the bath with water. I sat there for over two hours while the storm raged on. At some points, you would mutter things I didn't understand. You talked about skipping stones, a cat you saw, and maybe drugs. You looked so peaceful, and I stayed with you the whole time."

I had nothing to say to this, so I remained silent while looking at her. She sighed. "Once it had been a couple of hours, I got a towel for you and made sure you were warm and put you in your bed. Walking into your room, there were pills everywhere. I didn't even snoop or anything. You had white and tan pills lying on the ground with your wallet out. I could see hundreds of dollars in bills. I spent the whole night watching you sleep, wondering what had happened."

She looked to me as if for answers. I tried to get the words out, but they wouldn't come. I knew I'd have to force them.

"I'm a drug addict to these pills you saw, and I sell them to make money."

I couldn't believe I'd said that. Would she connect Thomas's stabbing, Lily's boyfriend's death, or Connor's disappearance with me because of it?

Instead, she had a peculiar look on her face. "Michael, I'm your girlfriend now. There's nothing wrong with that. We're in high school. Well, graduating. I'll be here to help you with what you go through."

I felt so high in that moment, as if I couldn't feel any pain, as if all my sins had been abolished. I leaned over to her, watching her brown eyes and blonde hair look at me. "I love you," I said as I pulled her in to kiss her. She kissed me back, and for the first time in as long as I could remember, something loosened in my chest. This girl, Nicole, was my guardian angel. I'd been taking her for granted.

After we pulled away, she asked, "So you're not mad I had to see you, you know." I grabbed her hand and told her I couldn't care less.

"You were taking care of me, and I love you for it." Smiling at her knees, then looking towards me, she said, "You can't just tell a girl you love her, you know. You have to mean it."

I nodded and responded. "I think I've been in love with you for a long time. I just never knew how to put it into words."

She grabbed my hand and gave me a quick kiss. I looked outside. "It's still flooded and raining. Do you want to stay here with me?"

Nicole looked at the wall, and I interjected. "You can sleep in the bed. It'll fit both of us. You don't have to sleep against the wall."

Nicole looked at my head and then my eyes. "Well, that's just an offer I can't refuse."

She climbed into bed with me and held my hand. Feeling her warmth against me was the most relaxing feeling in the world. Maybe things had to go wrong for them to go right. I'd had to overdose and almost die to find someone I loved. I soon fell asleep with the last thought on my mind being the taste of Nicole's lips as I fell into an abyss.

Unravelings

A couple of days had passed since then, and I was extra careful with my pill usage. My body had been returning to good health as I took walks and stayed outside. My late-night calls with Nicole made me happy before bed. All that was coming up was graduation and then prom. The end of school for me, and the beginning of a new life that I hoped to do better in.

All the things I'd done in the past, I could put behind me after today. I looked at myself in the mirror and moved my wavy hair to one side to try to make it look better. Yesterday, I'd grudgingly tried on the suit I had rented out for prom and graduation. Wearing it and looking at myself in the mirror, I felt good. I looked good. I had the looks, the money, and the girl. There was nothing that could get in my way.

After today, I wouldn't have to worry about the police, as people from school would be leaving, which would make investigations harder. It made me feel alive, in a way. Thomas had tried to hurt me, and I'd tried to help Lily, but she was ungrateful, so her boyfriend had to go, and Connor was a straight moron who would have hurt Nicole if he'd finished me off. I'd been justified in all that I did, and this would be the end of it.

I combed my hair and put the brush down, taking one more look at myself in the mirror. The bags under my eyes showed, and I could see a broken boy in front of me, someone I no longer recognized. Putting my hand to my cheek, I felt my skin to see if I was alive. I held it there while staring at myself, feeling the uncertainty of life.

When looking into my soul, I knew that I couldn't plan everything even if I tried my hardest.

Leaving the bathroom, I grabbed my wallet and my Lucky Strikes and headed outside to light one up. Nicole was picking me up at seven tonight, and I had no clue when I'd be home. I'd thought of leaving a note for my mom, but she'd seemed distant from me lately, which made me irrationally annoyed, so I didn't talk to her.

With Nicole coming in twenty minutes, I savored every drag and took three pills for tonight. I knew I would need absolutely zero anxiety and decided to treat myself. I took a long drag, thinking about everything that had happened to me recently. Why shouldn't I enjoy myself tonight? Why did I need drugs to compensate for my lack of life? These were stupid questions I would never know the answer to.

I crushed the cigarette under my foot and started walking around to get the smell off me. I wondered who I'd see there. I wondered if I'd have to dance. I wondered if I'd have to go on stage. I wondered until my brain hurt so bad that I punched the gate next to my house. My hand started to bleed, and as I was wearing a suit, I cursed at my stupidity. Failure.

Thinking about this, ironically, Nicole pulled up in her Camry.

"Michael?" she asked wildly as I held my right hand with my left, trying to cover it.

I told her I was good and asked if she had something to put on it. She hurried back towards her car. "Yes, I've got a shirt you can wrap around it."

God bless this girl. I thanked her and held up my hand as she wrapped it. Getting into the car, she asked me what had happened. I looked down at my hand, looking for an excuse. "I cut myself while trying to make a snack before I left."

I didn't know if she believed this, but she nodded. "I'm just glad it's not as bad as it looked at first. I would have missed prom to spend the night in the ER with you."

Did she mean that? I couldn't tell if a human could be this kind. Paranoia crept into my brain, but I was able to push it away.

As we drove to the school, I told her that her dress looked beautiful. She gave me a big smile. "My mom didn't want to wear it, but when I saw it, I threw my hands around it and knew I had to have it."

I'd just picked out the first option they'd given me. How funny life is. She kept talking. "Apparently, there will be supervisors there tonight to make sure no one's drinking or doing drugs. Something like that." I asked her if she meant cops.

"I'm not sure. It's just what my friends told me. They plan to do that stuff after prom regardless, though." Great. If the police were there, I was sure my brain would function at full capacity.

I knew I had to get through prom tonight and graduation tomorrow. As we got closer, Nicole motioned all around the school. "Aren't you going to miss all this?"

I wanted to laugh hysterically but gave her a simple yes. We walked in together as Nicole grabbed my left hand, while I put my damaged right hand into my coat pocket. If it got blood on it, I'd pay for the stupid thing in its entirety. "This way for entry pictures," a girl I recognized shouted. Our class president was running a booth where you took pictures with your prom dates. I could never smile in photos, and in my state of mind, trying felt impossible.

"Come on, let's go in and get our picture taken," Nicole said, pulling me over.

When we got to the booth, the class president thanked us for coming and spoke with Nicole briefly. I'd never talked to her, nor did I know her name, so I tried not to disturb their conversation. Their conversation came to an end, and I was pulled over to the picture booth.

"Three, two, one, say cheese!"

I tried my best to smile, and it turned out decent when it printed. I didn't know how I'd faked that, but I thanked my body as Nicole led us in.

I had zero clue what I was in for, so I asked her what we'd do. Nicole looked at me and squeezed my hand. "Whatever we want. It's our goodbye to school in a party sense."

School and I could have parted on not-speaking terms if I'd had my way. This was not the mentality I needed today, so I smiled and told her, "Okay. Let's get into it then."

Making our way into the gymnasium where it was held, songs were playing. I scanned the room to see if anyone I knew was here and to look for the "security" she'd mentioned. I saw a girl who looked an awful lot like Lily, which made me instantly want to vomit, but I turned around to see that there were actual police officers there. In the corner, I could feel someone's eyes on me. The devil that went by Officer Resen was staring directly at me. Was he waiting for me? Did Nicole bring me here for this? I needed a break. I told Nicole I needed to go to the bathroom and would meet up with her at the spot where she wanted to see her friends. "Be back quick," she said, waving at me.

I looked around for an exit to the outside, as I needed fresh air and a smoke. The night sky around me looked empty except for the stars and the buzz of people. My stomach dropped all over and tried to keep my head up, looking at the stars. I wanted to see those two stars again, but they weren't visible tonight. Perhaps I was at the wrong angle, I thought.

A door opened behind me, which I assumed was people walking by, so I held my smoke in. But the person behind me walked up, and I could hear them getting closer. They took a seat to the left of me at the table I was at. I blew my smoke to the right and looked at him, bored. "What can I do for you?" I asked in a monotone voice.

Officer Resen sat next to me, never taking his eyes off me. "You look stressed. Why aren't you inside partying?"

I knew he had nothing on me, which made this whole interaction annoying. I took another drag and told him I was watching the stars.

"Does that make you feel better about the things you've done? Are you trying to dissociate from what's happening around you?" he said slyly, his lips curling. I didn't know what he meant by this, but it triggered a response in my body that gave me extreme anxiety. This shouldn't be possible with the amount I'd taken, I thought.

I wanted to piss him off now and get away. I flicked the cigarette from my fingers. "I have no clue what you're talking about, Officer."

Resen looked at me and then up at the sky. "Connor has stopped showing up to talk about you. Interestingly enough, he's stopped showing up to school entirely."

I'd never mentioned Connor to him, nor had he to me. He was trying to catch me in a trap to see if I knew what he was referencing. Leaning on my right hand, I asked him who Connor was and what it had to do with me.

Resen put his hands on the table. "He was Thomas's friend who was convinced you had a part to play in what happened to him."

I put on a fake frown. "What happened to Thomas was truly a tragedy."

"Well, whatever the case, kid, Your name keeps coming up in places it shouldn't. The girl you brought tonight will be interviewed, and your other friend Lily's name came up many times during the interrogations. Interestingly enough, she said you guys stopped talking around this time."

I doubted he had any concrete evidence, and I tried to think of a response, but my anxiety was at an all-time high. I hid my hands under the table as they began to shake. I responded directly, facing him. "I have no intention of talking to you. Please leave."

"Well, be in contact sooner than you think, Michael," Resen said as he pushed out of his chair and walked away. I didn't care if he was watching me. I got up and speed-walked to the side of the school, where I threw up multiple times. I tried not to get my clothes dirty and got my wallet out to take five pills, one by one. The powder of them burned my tongue and made me want to gag, but there was nothing left. I had to get cleaned up.

Walking around to the front of the school, I could feel eyes all around me. I didn't know who to trust or what to do next. Was he bluffing, or did he have something on me? Every thought made me sicker. Making my way in through the front, I found the bathrooms where I washed my mouth out with water, repeatedly. The mirror above the sink was cracked as I stared into it.

What stared back at me was a version of me with only one eye on half my face, while the jagged edges of the mirror ran down the middle. Everything is broken, I thought. I snapped back and realized I'd left my prom date. I had no clue how much time had passed, but I knew it couldn't be good. Adjusting my tie, I walked back in past the class president, who tried to get my attention. My only goal was to find Nicole.

I spotted her friend group and walked over to them as they stood in a circle. As I got closer, I heard them talking about all the usual things I'd expect from these morons:

this boy, that boy, college, dorming, partying. When I was there, I spoke to no one in particular. "Could you guys tell me where Nicole is?"

One of her friends frowned and pointed over to the front of the stage.

My heart dropped. I saw Nicole talking to a slender girl with blonde hair. What was happening to me? I stopped because my nerves hurt so much, and my brain was telling me something was wrong. The officer, Nicole, and Lily were all here? Something was going on, and I was caught in the middle of my consequences. The only move was to walk over and talk to them. Forward, we only go. I had no doubt Officer Resen was watching me somewhere, and I needed my body to fucking move.

Hands in my pockets, getting ready to make an apology to Nicole and a greeting for Lily, my legs moved in their direction. I tapped Nicole on her shoulder and whispered in her ear before she had a chance to respond. "I'm sorry for leaving. It was my only choice at the moment."

Nicole didn't respond as she looked at me with a sad frown.

"Mikey, I can't believe you're here and you have a girlfriend!"

Lily said this in the cruelest way, which only made my head worse. If I'd had a gun in my pocket, I would have blown my brains out at that moment, as the pain was getting to be too much. She was making a game of this, knowing I'd kissed her and had feelings for her. I wondered if she'd told Nicole, which was why Nicole could have been sad.

All I could utter was, "Yeah, a lot has happened in the past week. I'm thrilled to be here with Nicole tonight, though."

Lie. Lie. Lie. I was tiring of lying. I hated being here. I had to lie for Nicole and myself. I grabbed Nicole's hand to test if she was mad, and she accepted it. Good. At least I had Nicole on my side. I could turn this around.

Suddenly, I had brain zaps. The benzo usage had been causing them, and I had to stand there while an invisible hand punched my brain over and over.

"You two are such a cute couple, Mikey. You should have told me," the blonde girl said.

I wanted to strangle her at that moment but resorted to words. "I probably would, but you've been going through so much and high constantly, so maybe you just forgot?"

Nicole shot me a look as if to say, What is going on here?

"Oh, please, don't pretend like you're a saint." She looked towards Nicole. "You know how many benzos he takes a day?"

Was she drunk, I wondered? What the fuck was she attacking me for? I couldn't believe this was the same girl I'd saved.

"Oh, and Mikey, the cops have been asking about you a lot. You should probably go talk to them and get it resolved." With a flip of her hair, Lily turned around to throw up a peace sign and walked off to join her friends.

As she walked away, I realized something in the way she moved. She didn't have that usual Lily confidence. I'd known her long enough to know when she was faking it. She never even looked back at me to see how I reacted.

No. I couldn't think that way. You have something good in your life for once. Don't fuck it up. You're overthinking it. Lily is fine. She's probably just tired.

Nicole had started to walk towards the stage to sit down in front of it. I grabbed her hand again. "I'm sorry.

Old friend. She's been erratic ever since her boyfriend died."

Nicole didn't look at me while responding. "She never mentioned having a boyfriend."

This was a completely robotic, monotone voice.

"She said some guy she knew was supposed to take her, but he like disappeared or something, so she just showed up alone."

Jesus Christ. I couldn't catch a fucking break. No wonder she didn't seem to care at all.

"A friend?" I replied, my voice cracking. She nodded, finally looking at me.

"Why do you look like you've been through hell and back? It's only been an hour," Nicole said innocently, sitting down, looking at me. I sat down next to her, burying my face into my arms so no one could see my tears. I hadn't saved Lily. I'd killed an innocent person and watched him suffer. In his last moments, I could have saved him, but I watched as his eyes rolled back. I didn't want to live. Everything about me was a broken, horrible mess. Every decision I made led to something bad happening.

I turned one eye out of my arms and pleaded. "Can we go far away from here?"

Nicole still had a distant look in her eye. Lily had told her something, and I couldn't probe her for what it was at the moment. In a dead voice, she responded, "Sure."

We left the building holding hands just as we had entered, but the warmth between our hands had gone cold, and all that remained was a severed connection held together only by the will of bones.

Realization

Sitting in the passenger seat watching the town fly by, I felt this overwhelming sensation. It was as if my anxiety, which I'd suppressed with pills, was trying to get out. I knew this was one of the lowest points of my life. At the moment, I didn't care that Nicole wasn't talking. I didn't want to exist. I didn't speak the whole time as we drove out of town.

I tried to think about what to do next. Normally my brain would lay it all out for me like a map. Go here, do this, say that. It always worked. I would run through every scenario until I found the one that kept me alive and ahead of everyone else.

But nothing was connecting. I started to plan what I would say to Nicole about tonight and lost the thought halfway through. I tried again and got further but then it slipped away like I was grabbing at smoke. What the fuck was happening to me? I blamed the pills and the amount I had taken tonight. That had to be it. My brain was just tired.

But I had taken more than this before and been fine. I stared out the window and tried one more time to think of a plan, any plan, and all I got was static.

"So right before we started dating, you were already interested romantically in this Lily girl?"

Nicole stared straight ahead at the road while saying this. I began to speak, to make up some lie, when my brain just said fuck it.

"Yeah. I've liked her for as long as I can remember," I told her, looking out the window in a flat voice. I wanted it all to come crashing down. Nothing good deserved to happen to me. I wanted more pain.

The darkness in front of us seemed to go as long as the silence in the car.

"I've loved you for a long time as well, Mikey," she said, one hand on the steering wheel and one hand on her face.

Loved? I didn't understand this and had to respond. "You can't love me. I am the definition of a broken man, Nicole. I'm being serious, too. The things I've done."

I ended it there, not wanting to say more. The more I spoke, the sicker I felt. Nicole hadn't moved and was still staring straight ahead. I waited for her to speak. Finally, she retorted. "You have to understand, when I'm with you, I feel like a whole different person. I feel warm when I'm with you. I don't care what you've done. I want you and only you. It sounds cheesy, and I hate hearing it come out of my mouth, but you're the only one I ever wanted."

I didn't respond, so she continued.

"When I heard Lily say all those things to me, I knew she was just jealous that I was with you. She's missed out and wanted to hurt me. I don't care what she did with you. As long as I'm with you, I'll be happy."

Never hearing this much emotion in my life, I struggled to find the right words. What she'd said had made my stomach turn, but in a nervous, excited way. I didn't think it was possible for a person to love me, but she'd made it clear she did. "I love you too, Nicole," was simply all I said.

After hearing this, she pulled off onto a dirt path and killed the ignition.

"Give me some of those pills you have," she said, looking directly at me. If it would make her feel better, I told her sure and gave her some. Swallowing them, she looked towards me and pulled me forward to kiss her. I felt the warmth of her all over my body. I wanted to stay like this forever.

She pulled off and motioned towards the backseat while taking off her shirt. I realized what was happening and thought to myself for one split second if this was trauma-induced, but my brain switched back as I took off my shirt and climbed into the back with her. We spent the next thirty minutes embracing each other in every way possible. I couldn't understand what I was feeling. Love? Lust? All I felt was good emotions pouring out of me everywhere while I stared down at her.

I was drifting off, as I'd taken my pills, and having taken over a dozen by tonight, I was beginning not to understand much of anything. Nicole wrapped her arms around my back. "Together, you and me, forever."

I nodded at her and fell into her chest. I was so tired that I began to drift and drift until the darkness around me became light once more.

Liberation Day

Graduation day was upon me. The end of school and the end of this chapter of my life. I went over to my mom and asked if she wanted to go, but found her asleep. Walking over to her, I kissed her on her forehead and told her, "I did it."

Walking out of the house to the school was what I wanted to do. One last time of walking. Nicole had texted asking if I needed a ride, but I told her I'd be good.

I couldn't remember much of the night before except the ending of it. The pills I'd taken had caused so much rebound anxiety. When I'd gotten up, I immediately had to take painkillers with Xanax. My batch of Xanax was down to twelve hundred. Two hundred for me and a thousand for Trey, who I'd see later tonight.

With all these thoughts in my head, I began to see the school surrounded by cars. It reminded me of town fairs I used to go to with my family. Everybody was out taking pictures with their mom and dad, and here I was strolling up alone in a white shirt and black pants. No mother or father to see me graduate. I wondered what my father would be thinking right now if he could watch. Would he have been proud of me? It didn't matter. The past was history, and he was long dead. Everything I did, I would be the sole recipient of.

Walking through the doors of the gymnasium gave me a sudden rush of panic, and I had to stop and lean against a wall. I saw a family staring at me, and I turned to stare back until they stopped. I was beginning to realize how fucked my memory was. It saddened me, but there was nothing I could do about it.

Being a Ren, I was towards the back of the men's line. I found my spot, filed into a group of people, and took my seat. I stared aimlessly at the podium while everyone around me talked, filled with joy and happiness. For me, this was a means to an end. For them, it was an experience of a lifetime. I hated the way they laughed, and I hated how they all talked together. No one here deserved that except for Nicole.

Nicole, Nicole, Nicole. My mind wandered as I sat there and thought about the night before. Together, you and me, forever. I'd relegated my emotions to nothing since my father died, but there was something about her that gave me hope. I wouldn't mind being with her forever. She didn't care what I'd done, and she loved me for me.

Snapping back to reality, I heard the first bunch of names called. Every single time someone went up, all their families clapped and yelled, which annoyed me as much as possible. Just be proud of them and move on. You don't have to act like they just graduated from fucking Yale. I zoned out, incredibly bored, until I finally saw Nicole go up.

A stunning black dress was on her, and her hair looked so blonde that I wondered if it was dyed. I felt my hands start to clap for her as she got her diploma. This girl had my mind wrapped in quicksand, and there was no escaping it. Any thought I had of her was jumbled. All I felt was the need to be with her. After she got off stage, I had to see one more familiar face.

As they called Lily to the stage, I stared in contempt. I didn't know how to feel about her in any regard. She was meaningless to me now, as I'd found someone who gave a singular fuck about me. The haunting truth was that I would always have to keep her close, as she knew what I'd done to Thomas. I wished I'd never done any of it. The more I thought about it, the more I realized this was all her fault. If I hadn't gone out that night for her, Thomas wouldn't have gotten hurt, which means Lily wouldn't have gone into depression and ended up with her drug-dealer boyfriend, and Connor would never have come after me. Stupid fucking bitch.

"Michael Ren."

There, my name was announced. I got up and proceeded to the stage where I took my diploma and shook the principal's hand. I tried to smile for the picture but couldn't manage one. Then it was over. All in one minute. How fast life can change.

Instead of returning to my seat and waiting for the others to finish, I walked down the aisle, hugging the wall, and left the school. There wouldn't be any after-parties with my friends or family. Nobody would be taking pictures of my mom and dad around me while I held my diploma up. There was nothing in this world for me there. I looked up to the clouds to see rain, but I felt a tear drop out of my left eye onto my diploma, hitting it right where it said "Ren." I was all alone.

Journal

On the last day of school, we handed in the journals we'd been writing all year. I hadn't written much, just thoughts here and there when I was sober.

Everyone would get up, hand their journals in, and walk out. I could hear them celebrating outside. Wow, you passed Honors English. Fucking morons.

"Ren."

I heard Mr. Wright call my name.

I walked up with my journal. Mr. Wright looked up at me while he held it but didn't open it.

"Michael, I've seen you all year in class, but everything in your journal completely contradicts the way you act."

I don't know if my face gave it away, but for a split second I was caught off guard. I asked him what he meant.

"What I mean is, I knew of your father and mother. You've gone through a lot. But you never write about that. You write about day-to-day things. A journal should be a place where you can talk about those things."

I told him I was fine and started to walk away slowly.

"Michael, seriously. I know something must be wrong. You're my last student. I know you're insanely smart. You never use the time in class to study or anything—"

I wanted to say something, but he interjected.

"Don't deny it. I see what my students do."

He paused.

"I get the feeling you're alone."

Why was he asking me all this? Why would a teacher care about this bullshit? I decided to play along. What did I have to lose anyway?

"Yes, I am alone. I've lost everything I care about in some sense or way. Nothing goes my way. Nothing."

He motioned over to me. "Sit down, Michael."

I walked over and sat in a chair facing him.

"I'm going to give you the number of the school counselor. I know you're graduating, but there are resources you can go to for this type of thing. Everyone goes through hard things in life. Maybe not as much as you, but they do."

I took the card he gave me with bitterness. I didn't need help from some fucking school counselor who would tell me that some therapy and medication might help. What would help me was if my dad didn't blow his brains out or my mother wasn't a fucking invalid.

"Michael, your silence tells me a lot. I know that you're going to have a bright future. This school will be your alma mater. Take care of the resources it gives you. And next time you journal, put the truth into it."

I got up and told him thank you, wanting to just be out of there and be done.

"You got this, Michael," he told me.

Those words cracked in my skull. My father had said the same thing. Maybe I was wrong. Maybe I should tell Mr. Wright everything, consequences be damned.

I heard my phone beep and looked at it. Text from Nicole. What was I thinking? I didn't have time for this.

"Thank you, Mr. Wright. It means a lot."

I turned to the door and walked out. I saw the gate to leave the school, and as I walked, I read the card with the guidance counselor's number on it. I fidgeted with it before I flicked it into the wind.

Only I can help myself.

Planning

With summer approaching, I had to plan for what the next couple of months would entail. Being all alone, knowing I had nothing to back me up while I was being chased down, was not a pleasant feeling. I'd stopped at the local gun store in town and finally bought a firearm. My knife wouldn't be able to protect me forever.

When I was there, I wanted something fast with no recoil, and the man led me to buy a .22 revolver. When I'd purchased it and loaded it with ammo, I was able to hide it in my sweater or the back of my pants. It had that Clint Eastwood feel to it. As I lit up a cigarette near the water tower, carrying it made me feel like I wasn't alone.

Trey was late today, which was unusual since this was a large batch I was selling. I'd half expected James to show up in his place, but that didn't happen. I waited for hour after hour until I decided to go looking for him. I went down the path he always took, which led to the outskirts of town. Asking people about where he was would draw unwanted attention I didn't need.

Going down the block, I encountered nobody for an extended period until a straggler who looked to be smoking something other than weed appeared when I got to the street. I snapped my fingers to see if he was conscious, to which he looked at me with glossy eyes.

"Do you know where I can find Trey?"

The man looked at me and pointed left.

"That doesn't help me. Could you at least tell me what his house looks like?"

The man ignored me and went back to smoking. I took out my wallet and threw a hundred dollars at his feet. "If you know where he is, this is yours."

The man scooped up the money so fast and looked at me with crazy eyes that almost made me stumble backwards. "Black Camaro," he said, pointing to the left.

Believing that was all I was going to get, I told him thank you, but he didn't reply. I went in the direction the man was pointing, looking for a black Camaro. It would stand out like an eyesore in this part of town. This place was a shithole, and he owned a fucking Camaro? I didn't have time to think about the stupidity of my drug-connection decisions as I walked until I saw it. Three houses down from me, I saw a house with two cars, including a black Camaro.

I made sure my gun was in the back of my pants and the drugs in my sweater pocket and walked towards his house. What an odd, deserted place this was. It felt like someone's dream of a town that was dead, yet still habitually residential. If he was making so much money, why would he live here? Too many fucking questions in my head, I thought, rubbing my eyes as I got to his door.

I gave three soft knocks and was greeted by a raspy "Who is it?"

I responded, "Michael," because why the fuck not at this point. The person who opened the door looked skinny and almost like a freak from a horror movie.

"You here to buy?" Annoyed, I told him I was checking if Trey was home.

"Yeah, come in. Just keep your voice down. Ma is asleep." His mother was here? Were these two related?

That would explain the two cars. The freakish-looking man went upstairs, presumably to grab Trey.

Waiting, I walked back and forth, debating whether to sit on the couch, but the image of Trey seeing me sitting on his couch seemed like bad optics. Finally, I heard people coming down the stairs, grumbling. Trying to catch what they were saying, all I could make out was something along the lines of "looks like him."

I wondered if the freakish guy didn't like how I looked or something.

Trey finally emerged with him. "I see you've met my brother Joseph."

Ah, that was this guy's name. Joseph was practically jumping up and down. "He looks just like him, don't you see?"

Trey told him to leave us, while I was left wondering who the fuck I looked like.

"I got your delivery for you," I said, placing the thousand Xanax on the table.

Trey winced at this and shook his head. "We can't do business anymore."

My heart sank. This was all I had. All I could think of to say was "Why?"

He looked around the house and up the stairs, where I assumed Joseph was. "The police have been coming around here lately and talking to people. Your name has been brought up way too many times."

My chest was pounding. I could still salvage this, though. "What about James? Could I sell to him?" I asked desperately.

Trey shook his head. "He didn't want to be around you. Seeing what had happened to your father."

What?

"What did you just say? Like, can you tell me what you mean, please?" I said, feeling a panic attack starting to rise.

Trey looked at me uncomfortably, hesitating. "It's better if we stay on topic."

Angered by this, I shouted at him. "No, what the fuck do you mean? What happened to my father?"

He looked at me, grabbed the Xanax, and took me outside by the arm. "Put these in your damn sweater."

We stood outside facing each other.

"I didn't think this would ever be brought up, but if you want to know so bad, James was a friend of your dad's who used to sell to him. Got mixed up with some bad people. Never saw your dad again after that. James realized you looked exactly like him and freaked out. Didn't want to meet with you again."

Not knowing how to process this with my heart racing, I tried to breathe. My back faced him as I asked who these bad people were.

"Information like this isn't free, but I feel bad for you, kid, and you've helped me a lot. Last name's Lillan. That's all I've got for you."

Lillan. Trey reached out to shake my hand. "It was good to work with you, and if you need the money, you can sell to people on the street and make a lot more."

I stood there, not shaking his hand. "Why can't you?"

Saddened, which I thought was an emotion this man could not show, he told me his mother was sick. Nothing I could do there. I shook his hand and thanked him for the help. Before I turned to leave, he spoke. "One last piece of advice. Stay off the radar and don't do anything stupid."

Like I didn't already fucking know that. "Thank you, Trey," I said, waving to him as I walked off.

As soon as I was out of sight, I reached in and grabbed a couple of bars to mitigate my panic attack. I couldn't go back to my house with these if people had been asking around. The cops could be waiting at my house right now for all I knew. Grabbing my phone, I dialed Nicole and told her I was on the outskirts of town. "Why are you over there? Do you need me to pick you up?" I told her if it were convenient, to which she replied she'd be there soon.

I was beyond fucked in every regard. I thought about pulling my gun out and blowing my brains out right then and there. Like father, like son. But I decided against it. I knew someone had wronged my dad in some way, and I still had to keep the house so my mom wouldn't end up on the street. I was strictly living for other people at this point in my life, as my own life held no value unless it was to help others. All I did was help others, and look where it got me. Life is fucking moronic. I would change this. I wouldn't shoot myself. I wouldn't stop making money. I would have a good relationship with Nicole. And I would find out who this Lillan was.

Default

After a lengthy explanation to Nicole that I needed her to keep this package in her house for the time being, she seemed to agree.

"I love these pills, so if I can use one once in a while, I'll do it for you."

I'd told her to go for it. I needed them out of the equation.

"My mother never checks my room, and my dad is never home, so they'll be fine with me."

I'd thanked her and watched as she opened up her closet and hid them in a pile of clothes behind a bunch of drawers.

Nicole seemed satisfied and asked if I wanted to do anything today. Wishing I could, I told her I had to go to the bank and pay off the rest of my mother's house. "What a gentleman you are," she replied, kissing me.

"Do you need a ride?"

I told her I'd be okay and thanked her.

"Just call me when you're done."

Telling her I would, I left the house and started for mine.

I walked towards my house with thoughts swirling through my head. Everything would be fine. I'd arrive at home, get the rest of the money I had to pay off the house, and tell my mother.

When I entered the house, I realized how terrible I felt about my father. I didn't want to ask my mother, but I wanted to see her. Not like I was going to brag about paying off the house, I just needed my mother for once.

Arriving at my house, I went into my mother's room. With all I'd been through, I needed to hear her voice. I walked in and saw her. Her body was on the bed, lifeless, and she stared at the ceiling with her eyes wide open.

"Mom?"

I moved closer to see what she was doing. Her eyes met mine. "Mikey," she trailed off as she placed a hand to my face. She seemed sober, even though she wasn't moving. "Mikey, if only your father could see you right now. He'd be so proud of you."

I hated that she said that. "No, you're wrong, Mom. I hate myself. There, I said it. I hate myself, and you weren't fucking there for me. Look at me, Mom."

My mother was staring at me now, and it was like looking at the old her. Before everything went wrong. "Michael, I wasn't able to take care of you after he passed."

I was on the verge of tears. "But you could have just fucking tried. Instead, you lay in bed all day while I have to pay off the house. Every time I thought about coming in here, you were high. I needed someone in my life, Mom. It's all fucking gone."

She looked towards the ground. "I'm proud of your graduation, Michael. I wasn't able to be there, but it made you into the man you are today. I love you."

My eyes began to drip tears. "I wish you could have been there, mother."

She spoke up again. "From now on, I can try harder. Since you paid off the house, I'll be up more. I promise."

I didn't believe her. "How can you promise such a thing? After all you've done."

She looked at me again. "Because I'm your mother, Michael."

I got up. I had to go anyway. "Thank you, Mom. I love you too. And I do hope you keep that promise."

Before I reached the door, I noticed an old photograph of our family. My mom had laid back down and was staring at the ceiling as I looked over, so I picked it up.

It was of all three of us at the baseball stadium. I was the spitting image of my father. No wonder James had recognized me so quickly. I remembered this game because Lily had tried to go for a triple and got tagged out before my game, and she was angry about it.

Looking closer at my dad, I realized I'd never looked at any photos of him since he died. He had such a nice smile, something I apparently did not have. And my mother with his arm around her looked so happy. I held the photo to my chest. I wished I could jump into the picture and relive this day. Looking over at my mom and then back towards the photograph. Where did it all go wrong?

I knew I had at least twenty grand saved up, which would pay it off in full. I decided this was the best course of action, as it would give me a roof to sleep under and my mother wouldn't have to worry about it. It was the right thing to do, and I needed a house if I wanted to go on. Calculating in my head how much I'd have left, I was granted a number around three grand, which seemed like enough. For a moment, I was proud of myself. Getting out my wallet and popping another pill while drawing a cigarette, I thought that maybe everything would be all right. In total, I took the amount the bank had asked for. A measly 3 grand compared to 20 grand. I would use the 17 to pave my own way.

If I had my own house, I could clean it up, get my mom help, and maybe even have Nicole over. These all felt like silly dreams, but at the same time, they seemed doable. I just needed to be vigilant and move forward. Leaving my street, I heard the blare of a siren and lights. I wondered for a split second if my mom had finally overdosed. I was all alone anyway.

My curiosity got the better of me. I headed back to my house. This was too much activity for me to be out the loop.

Getting closer, I realized it wasn't ambulances. To my horror, it was police cars. Around my house, where I went in and out through the front door. I ran up to the nearest car to get a better look at the scene. An officer was standing next to a squad car, and I walked up and told him this was my residence.

"We're just collecting evidence and cleaning up some things," he replied nonchalantly, like it was just another day. I rushed past him into the house to try to find my mom. I had just talked with her twenty minutes ago.

I called out to her, but all I found were two officers who came from my kitchen.

"Are you Michael Ren?"

I nodded yes.

"We're here to confiscate any drugs and book your mother into a mental facility."

This made no sense to me. The anger could be heard in my voice as I spoke. "What drugs, and you're not taking my mother away."

The officer seemed to find this amusing and told me, "It seems she's had quite a few more bottles of drugs than she was prescribed and has been making money off of it."

What the fuck was he talking about?

Disengaging from this, I went to my room to get my money and check for my belongings, but there were none. I stared at the empty drawer where I'd kept it in disbelief. Moving slowly now, I wobbled over to my nightstand and opened the drawers to see if any of my pills remained. Everything was gone. In a state of shock, I walked down to my mother's room to find it thoroughly cleaned out. No drugs and her gone.

Were they waiting for me to leave? It all made sense now. My mother promising me. An empty promise. They had been watching and trying to catch me in the act. How could it have come to this? They cleaned out my house so fast. So many thoughts rushed through my head. I needed plans, but I gave up on thinking as my brain melted.

I crumbled onto her bed and hugged her pillow, trying to smell her scent. Why was all this happening to me? Why was I alone again? They had taken everything from me. I looked around the room, taking in the surroundings, thinking, This is how my mother saw life for the past year.

This reminded me that I needed to find her. As I regained my senses, I rushed downstairs to find officers and ask where she was. One of them pointed towards a squad car, and I ran over to it.

The window was down, and she looked ghastly sick.

"Mom, what's happening?" I asked in a quiet tone. She looked at me and grabbed the side of my cheek with a sad smile.

"Mikey, I'm proud of you, no matter what you do. I'm sorry I couldn't keep my promise."

I grabbed her other hand. "Thank you, Mom, but none of that matters anymore. They're going to take you away? I don't know what's going on."

A rough voice behind me stepped into the conversation. "She is being transported to a facility in Northern California for mental health issues due to the drug usage."

I released my hands from my mom and looked at him angrily. "You have no right to do that in any way. She is fine."

The officer laughed at this and told me to get a move on. I looked towards my mother again. She looked back at me. "I'll be home soon, Mikey. It's for the best. You're the man of the house now, so make your father proud. And know your mother already is."

I ran towards her to grab her hands and reached her as she kissed me on the forehead. I could feel the tears in my eyes, and I didn't care if the officers thought I was weak. This was unlawful, and this was my mother.

"I'll come get you soon, Mom. I promise. I love you."

Pulling on a strand of my hair, she told me, "I love you too, Michael."

I was told to get out of the car as the window was rolled up. I watched in disbelief as the car turned on its engine and slowly drove away. I watched every second of it until it was out of view. I replayed it over and over in my head. She was gone, and I remained.

Not knowing what to do, I walked back to some of the remaining officers and asked about the money situation. I explained that the money was mine, not hers.

"You can have it back when we understand what fully happened here. We suspect it was drug money and needs to be held for evidence until your mother, in a clean mental state, can claim it," the officer told me in a rough tone.

I wanted to argue, to scream at him that he was a fool and how I'd worked my ass off for that, but something in me just made me say, "Okay."

I didn't have anything else left in me. The street I wandered down didn't look real. My thoughts felt fake, and my body hurt from the pain I'd experienced. They'd dragged my mother away like she was a criminal. Was this my fault? Failure. I slapped myself in the face as hard as I could to get my brain back on track. I needed somewhere to go, and I only had one place.

I walked to Nicole's house, which took me quite a while. I had none of my belongings, some cash on me, my .22, and pills. I had no plan for life anymore. For a moment while walking, I again considered pulling the gun out and blowing my brains out, as the purpose of my life had ceased to exist. For some reason, I remembered my own words. Forward. If my life were going to be hell, I might as well walk the path. If the world wanted to go against me, I would stare back at it and laugh. I would never give up.

Lost

I sat in Nicole's bedroom as I recounted the story of everything that had happened. She embraced me, hugged my back, and told me how sorry she was. I'd heard sorrys all my life after my father passed. Every single time I'd hated them, as the people saying them had never and would never experience the pain I'd gone through. However, Nicole felt genuine, and I leaned back into her arms. I looked up at the ceiling, lying on my back. "Nicole, what the fuck do I even do anymore?"

She shifted around the bed to look at me. "We'll figure it out. You're still here and we're together. Remember? Together, you and me, forever."

Forever. I repeated the sentence in my brain over and over.

"I'll ask my parents if you can stay here for the time being," Nicole told me. "I'm sure she'll understand what you're going through, and I've already told her so much about you that she'd have to say yes."

I thanked her and thought this over. My chances of buying a house were surely gone now that I didn't have the money to pay it off. I could stay here for a bit until I figured out how to sell the Xanax I was hiding here. I asked Nicole if she still had it, to which she responded, "Yeah, although I admit I've been taking a couple for when I'm alone and bored. Don't be mad, please."

She said this in such a sweet voice that I reassured her it was fine and she could use them anytime, as she was doing me a big favor.

In my mind, I thought about how little Xanax I'd been taking. Maybe my body was weaning off them. Pain still lingered in my body, but Xanax wouldn't help that. I knew how to fix it, but that was a last resort I preferred not to take. Nicole leaned over, telling me she was considering taking a gap year to stay here and work. I told her that was what I was going to do, which made her smile. "We can do it together, then," she said happily. The difference was that she had a choice, and I didn't.

I rolled over and let my mind wander into places that couldn't seem to be reached. I had no realistic plans in motion, and without a solid base, I couldn't create a future. I could cling to Nicole, but that wouldn't get me far. I needed something to take the pain away. I told her I needed to take a walk outside to clear my head, and she nodded. "Just be home safe." I told her I would and left for a terrible place.

Flipping open my phone, I hit speed dial, which redirected me to Lily. "I knew you'd come back to me after she left."

I sighed. "It has nothing to do with that. I need painkillers, and I have money. Do you have them?"

Lily laughed and told me of course, to which I hung up. Walking towards her house, I knew I wanted to be in and out as fast as I could. No talking to Katrina and no small talk with Lily.

I'd taken this route more times than I could count. Left on her street, right at the stop sign, straight until the blue mailbox. I could do this blindfolded.

Except I was standing at the intersection and couldn't remember if I went left or right. I stood there like a fucking idiot staring at two streets I had known my entire life. My brain was telling me both directions were correct. My heart started to race as I looked around to see if anyone was watching me stand there frozen.

My body started walking before my brain figured it out. My legs knew the way even if my head didn't. Even when I was at my lowest, I could still get it done.

Thankfully, when I arrived, Lily was already outside and tossed me a bag. "Fifty for a hundred pills," she told me confidently. Opening my wallet, I gave her a hundred and turned to leave. However, I heard her run up and grab my arm. Spinning around, I saw her looking at me like a small child, all the confidence and happiness erased from her face. I didn't have time for games.

"Oh, what is it already?"

She shook her head. "My mom's sending me to some rehab camp away from here. She thinks I need help and to get better, but I want to stay here." She grabbed my arm. "Don't let them take me."

Well, they'd already taken my mom today, and now she was going to be "taken," so for some reason my brain sympathized.

In a sweeping decision, I grabbed her and kissed her on the lips for as long as she would let me. We stood there like an inseparable bond, the earth and the moon. I wanted Lily in every way so badly.

"I won't let them take you. I promise. Just let me take these pills, get my head right, and I'll call you."

Lily looked dazed and put up three fingers.

"Days?" I said. She nodded.

"I'll have it figured out by then. I'll come get you tomorrow or the next day."

I turned to leave and was given one last gift. A small note that had been folded multiple times. I looked at it. "I'll read this when I'm home."

She agreed, and I went on my way. Instead of going to Nicole's, I decided to go to my police-raided house to avoid dealing with anyone. I was cracking under the pressure of everything happening so quickly and needed to be alone to think. I didn't love Lily. I loved Nicole. Did I love her? What was wrong with me?

Needing no key, I turned the knob on my door, got in, locked everything, and made my way up to my empty room. In a nihilistic sense, the room felt more like me

with everything gone. Now it had gone through
everything I'd gone through. It was all alone. Getting into
my bed, I remembered the note. A year ago, I would have
been brimming with excitement the whole way home, but
I hadn't even thought about it once. It could be blackmail
about what I'd done to Thomas, or her working with the
police.

Unfolding the note carefully, I saw it was on lined
paper stained pink and written with black ink.

Michael,

*I treated you the way I did because I was jealous,
plain and simple. I can't apologize for what I've done
because I know you, and you don't care about that. We
had this plan together to sell drugs and make money here,
and everything went wrong because of that stupid night,
and I'm sorry. I'm sorry for all that you've been through,
and I'm sorry for saying sorry because I know you hate
that too. I cannot imagine a life without you. I don't want
to be sent away and never see anyone I know again. We
became friends in the first place because we were the
social outcasts. I've come to learn that even when I was
on drugs and now that I'm sober, I am in love with you. I
know you've always liked me, but I never deserved it. If
I'm gone and you can't find me, keep this with you so a
piece of me stays with you forever. Please save me.*

Lily

I got out my phone and texted her immediately. I'll be
there tomorrow to pick you up and pack your things. I
didn't think I was falling for a trap, and if I was, what did

it matter? What more could I possibly lose? I needed a car, so I ran to the garage and found it was still there. An old Honda Civic that was as reliable as you could get.

I needed to figure out what to tell Nicole and get the drugs from her house. I could tell her I was going to see my mother and make sure everything was in order. She couldn't find out about this, as I needed Nicole in my back pocket. Simply put, I didn't have any intention of hurting her, and the thought made my brain saddened with despair. I was stuck inside a chasm that I led forward, but I always went backwards. If only I could override my emotions, maybe things would be different.

I packed up everything I needed. Not much, since the house had been raided, but I had clothing and my bayonet, which they hadn't taken. My revolver was still on me, and I threw that in my backpack too. I rushed downstairs to get the keys to the Civic and ran to the garage. There was no time to waste. My mind was an absolute mess, a beast screaming on the ground that had its legs cut off. I was stuck and could only resort to options of despair. If I couldn't save myself, I could save Lily.

I fired up the engine and watched as the garage door opened. Everything was in place and planned. I didn't know why I was so nervous. I started getting panic attacks in my chest and banged the wheel with my fists over and over. Leave me alone. I pulled out my wallet, crunching the pills so I had to deal with the terrible taste as a fuck-you to my body and mind. If I could get out of here with Lily and the pills, I could start over. Maybe I could even save my mom.

My father had never let me drive, only on special occasions, but luckily this was an automatic, so I didn't think it would be hard as long as I didn't get pulled over once I was out of this damn town. God, that would be a nightmare. I had no identification to show who I was. Did I even exist from the government's perspective?

I drove out onto the street, heading to Nicole's. It would be a minute's drive, and everything seemed to work in the car. I turned the radio off and made sure I could concentrate. I pulled up to Nicole's house, entered the driveway, and pushed the car into park. Hopping out, I had so many excuses for what to say in my brain that I wanted to bang my head against the door when I knocked. I looked around and saw more cars than usual on the street. Two white cars with strange-looking rearview lights. Just my paranoia, I thought. Don't be such an idiot.

Knocking on her door, I waited for about a minute. I was on the cusp of ringing the doorbell when the door opened, and I was face to face with Officer Resen.

"Hello, Michael. We're going to need you to come to the station," he told me with a smile as the cold handcuffs locked around my arms.

Confusion

"Do you know why you're in here?" the first cop asked me, whose name was Officer Logan. I guessed he was the chief, but I was never going to call him that. I was sitting in an interrogation room, feeling the cold all around me. The cold was probably on purpose to put me on edge, but what was making me shiver was that I didn't have any pills on me. My wallet had been confiscated, and my car had been towed. I had no clue if they'd found my gun. I also didn't know why the fuck I was in here.

I folded my hands. "Bad luck, I guess."

The chief was trying to do the age-old good cop, bad cop, because right next to him sat Resen. If I'd had my gun on me, I would have shot his smug ass right then and there. Resen talked next. "Look, we know what you did and what you've been doing. If you cooperate with us, everything will be fine."

Well, bullshit first off, and second, I didn't know what I was in here for. The only positive I could think of was that they didn't have information that I'd hurt anyone, or I'd already be in a cell.

Looking towards the ceiling in a bored manner, I ignored his statement. "When will I be able to leave legally?"

I knew they could only hold me for twenty-four hours if they had nothing on me. Thanks, Mom, for watching all those dumb crime shows when I was younger. Resen was quick to respond. "Whenever you start admitting what you've done. Now, where were you getting them from?" My mind started to convulse. Getting them. I thought to myself, please don't tell me what I think this is. "The pills, Michael."

I looked at him blankly, not registering any of this. Everything was gone. There was no point in talking to him. I clutched my stomach and looked up at the chief. "I'd like to speak to my lawyer and will not be talking anymore in this interrogation."

Not saying anything, the two of them looked at each other and left the room. Think. Think. Think. If I could get my lawyer here, I could spend the night, worst case, and post bail. I still had hundreds on me, or I could use the bail bond services. The latter seemed the better choice if I could get to that point, as I needed all the cash I had.

My lawyer entered the room and introduced herself as Ms. Magnellan. I told her I needed to be out of here as soon as possible. Watching her movements, she sat down at the table to my right and pulled out a file.

Ms. Magnellan opened her file and started talking at me like I was supposed to care about legal terms. Possession with intent to distribute. They had matched the Xanax at Nicole's to the shit they took from my house. So they knew it was all connected. Wonderful.

Then she told me Nicole had cooperated. Told them I hid the drugs there without her knowing. I wanted to be pissed at her but what was the point. I had told her on the phone to put it all on me. She did what I said for once.

The police really had done their homework on me. I wondered how long this little operation of theirs took. I felt bad for getting Nicole in trouble, but I was fucked even more. My mother gone, my drugs gone, my money gone, and I still had to save Lily. Jesus Christ. Oh, and yeah, I had to get out of jail. Little part I forgot.

I dosed off on what my lawyer was saying until the end where she mentioned house arrest. The ankle monitor was the part that got my attention. They were going to strap one on me before I walked out of here. I asked her straight up if they could track where I went. She looked at me like I had asked the dumbest question she had ever heard and told me yes, within city limits, and if I crossed the boundary it would send an alert to the station.

I shut up after that. Within city limits. Alert to the station. I didn't need to ask how fast that alert reached an actual person. I would figure that part out myself.

"The prosecutor has made a plea deal for the time being. If you post bail and agree to house arrest for the next thirty days while your case is investigated, you can get out of here."

I told her instantly that I would take that deal. I'll never forget how she looked at me with her eyes. She had probably seen a hundred people just like me, so desperate to get out that they'd jump at the first chance.

She passed over the paperwork, and I saw my bail was two thousand dollars. I asked if she could call a bond dealer to pay the ten percent, and she agreed. I signed my name and passed everything back. Getting up to leave, she looked over at me. "This is a generous offer, given what you've done. Be wise about it."

Sure, lady, whatever. I thanked her and was alone again.

Alone. I was always alone. I should have been driving to Lily's with the pills, but they were all gone. The withdrawals were going to kill me. I only kept about thirty in my wallet. Thinking of what to do, I realized Lily probably had painkillers, which I could take daily, while taking a fraction of a Xanax to supplement my body with a bit of alprazolam. I would have seizures, no doubt, but I could survive. And if I didn't? It didn't matter anymore. I was completely broke.

Chief Logan entered the room after a while of me sitting and flexing my hand. Looking down on me, he told me I was free to go, and my bail had been posted. I started to get up and headed out. The woman at the front told me that under no conditions was I to leave my house for thirty days unless I called for approval, for instance to get groceries. A squad car would patrol my house a couple of times a day and check in with me. Having no idea if this was all true, I nodded and agreed, as my mind was elsewhere.

Getting my belongings back, my hand reached for the inside of my wallet as I was sweating and my heart was pounding, but I was able to stop myself. I got my keys and was directed to where my car had been towed. Reaching it, I saw my backpack had been untouched, which was a sight for sore eyes. Once I had it, I put my head on the wheel and let out a sigh. The same wheel I'd been punching now felt like heaven to rest my head on.

I got a knock on my window, which, to my surprise, was the chief, who told me to drive home and follow the conditions of the plea. I couldn't think of anything better, so I did that. I went home, watching the empty roads and the dark sky in front of me. Was this the last chance I would have at freedom? It all seemed so up in the air.

Mulling it over, I realized I'd have to call Lily and explain why I wasn't there. Also, I wanted answers from a certain someone on why all my pills were gone and now I was under house arrest. If you want something done right, do it your fucking self. I hated how incompetent people were. I wouldn't be in any of this mess if Nicole hadn't been found out. Her mom was probably putting away clothes and stumbled on the stash. Such fucking stupidity, I thought.

Reaching home, I parked the car and closed the garage. I left the engine on and sat in the car. I was so exhausted, and I thought, Why not? Why not go to sleep and never have to deal with life again? This was the least painful way out. My body yearned for sleep, but my right hand jumped at the ignition and killed it. Somewhere deep inside my soul, I still wanted to live.

Far Away

That night, I lay in bed drifting in and out of consciousness. Lights flooded all around me as I lifted into my thoughts. Images of people floated around, talking to me about things I couldn't understand. I would break in and out of sleep to see if I was awake, then fall back into a pit of misery. Two birds encircled me as I stood in the darkness, a rope hanging between their teeth. Glowing as it got longer, it looped around me until I saw them fly away and was left holding it. A beacon of hope.

Daybreak hit my window soon after. Looking at it, I sighed, not finding the strength to get out of bed. Why keep going? My heart was racing, and I reached over to my drawer to find it empty. Of course. I couldn't lie down and feel sorry for myself forever. I had a job to do.

With the withdrawals grinding my brain, I walked downstairs and saw the time was three in the afternoon. I got my phone out and texted Lily. Sorry for not being there yesterday. Pack everything you need and be ready tonight at nine. Essentially, what I was doing was incredibly stupid and jeopardized my future, but as I looked around my empty house, I asked myself, What future? My mother was locked away in a mental facility, and my father was dead. I was the only one in this house, and soon it would be gone too.

Putting my head down on the table, I let myself cry. The consequences of my actions had all accumulated to this, and yet I couldn't take it. All I could do was run away. Up north, I knew they had secluded areas and the most beautiful beaches. I could picture it right now, sitting at the beach up north, the wind rustling my hair, watching the waves creep up on me, recede, and crash down.

Everything I needed to pack was done, and all I needed was a bit of luck that a police officer wouldn't check my house around nine. If I could get an hour head start, I'd be far away. Lily and I could start over, start from zero. Freedom. I dreamed of it. Alone in the woods watching the animals, small towns, going down to the beach and touching the water. This town had turned on me, and there was nothing left except misery and pain.

Having nothing to do until eight, I sat on the couch and set an alarm for the designated time. My mind wandered into unknown areas as I lay there. I was still just a kid, and I'd done terrible things. I'd burn in hell for what I'd done. If hell was eternity, the least I could do was spend my limited time on earth being free. I looked over to my right and saw a family photo of my mother and father standing next to me when I first started elementary school. We all looked so happy. No one could have guessed it would end this way.

"I'm sorry, Mother. I'm sorry, Father," I said to the picture as I curled up on the couch.

If there was ever a chance to set things right or get my life a glimmer of hope, this was the time. Hope was more potent than any drug I'd ever taken. It was always there, and you could try over and over again to get what you wanted and still have it. It would break most men, as it seemed to be breaking me, but I had to hold onto a sliver of it. The hope I possessed could lead me to a better life.

Connect

My phone buzzed in my hand, and as I stared at it groggily, I could make out the time. 8:30. No time like the present, I thought as I got up and grabbed my bag. I sent a quick text to Lily. Be ready. Then I walked through my house one last time. I moved my hands against the walls as I went into my room and then to my parents'. Staring at the bed where I'd found my father dead and watched my mother dying, I went over and lay down on it. "I hope you're still with me. I love you," I told them.

I forced myself up. There was no time for this. I was shoving clothes into my bag when I noticed I had put the same black shirt in there three times. I pulled all three out and stared at them like they were going to explain themselves to me. I could have sworn I only grabbed it once.

I looked at the clock. 8:30. I kept packing and checked the clock again. 8:30. That couldn't be right. I had been packing for at least twenty minutes. I checked my phone to see if the clock on the wall was broken, but my phone said the same thing. Either time had stopped or my brain had.

I took more pills. Not because they would fix anything. I just had nothing left to make me feel literally anything.

Before I left, I knew if I cut the monitor, I'd only have a small window, but that was all I needed. I grabbed whatever was left in the food pantry and threw it in with the rest.

I made sure everything in the house that I cared about would be taken, which frankly wasn't a lot. I grabbed my mom's pills and alcohol. While doing this, I saw the photograph I had found of us in her room. I stared at it again and put it in my bag.

Getting this thing off would be easy, I supposed. If scissors didn't work, the bayonet sure would.

Since I was grabbing my stuff to go, I had the bayonet on hand and told myself I was ready. I sliced at it upward and it cut off and began to blink red. No time like the fucking present. Forward we go.

After that, I ran to close off most of the lights except my bedroom to avoid suspicion and threw my stuff in the car. I had three-quarters of a tank of gas, which I assumed would get me around three hundred miles. More than I could ask for. Holding my breath, I opened the garage door and was met with an empty view. I hesitated with the keys at the ignition before taking a deep breath and firing it up. I drove up to the driveway slowly and closed the garage door behind me. I looked around to see if anyone was monitoring me, but I couldn't see anyone. The time on the car read 8:49, and I took a deep breath. Now or never. No more hesitations.

I drove the car slowly with the lights off to Lily's house, remarking to myself how oddly quiet it felt. It wasn't paranoid quiet. It was more of a peaceful feeling, which helped calm my racing heart. Driving down the street, I saw her outside with a suitcase. I quickly pulled over and popped the trunk. She understood and tossed it in. She got into the passenger seat, and we were off.

I knew what roads to take to go north and followed the back roads. Lily didn't say much at first until she managed to break the silence with a simple "Thank you."

Driving in the dark, I finally turned on my lights and was able to see her. "Of course. I'm just sorry I couldn't have been here earlier. I got wrapped up with the police, and they took my pills."

She had a concerned look on her face. I talked before she could respond. "How many painkillers do you have on you?"

Lily looked down and said she had some heroin and about twenty-five pills. Fuck.

Staring at the road and sky, the stars shone so bright. I thought back to that night when I'd seen those two stars so close together. Holding the wheel with one hand and taking Lily's with my other, I asked if she knew where we could get a bunch of painkillers. She nodded but asked, "Why?"

I told her I needed them to mix with the low amount of benzos I had so I wouldn't have withdrawals and die. She seemed to understand and told me she knew a guy who had sold to Lucas. Pills and heroin.

"I know where he lives, and it's only a bit west of here, if you have any money."

We were pretty much as far west as you could get, so I wondered where he could be, but decided I needed the pills more. She spoke again. "This guy's a real hardass. Let's hope we deal with his son and not him. The Lillans are an evil type of people."

I felt a shiver run down my back as she uttered those words. I slowed the car to a stop and pulled over. "Lillans?"

She looked at me as if I were crazy and said yes.

"What is it, Mikey?" she asked. I gripped the steering wheel, feeling the blood rush to my head. Could it be a coincidence? I doubted it.

"Nothing. I was just having withdrawals. Let's go to the place," I said as I turned the car back onto the road.

Driving down the road and listening to Lily give me directions had us lost for quite a while.

"I swear it's around here. It only used to take me thirty minutes out of town to get there," she said, looking dejected. Not thinking straight, all I could imagine was what would happen if I found this person who had known my dad. If in some way he'd contributed to my father's death.

"Okay, just try your best to remember. Let's keep going west until we see lights or you see a landmark," I told her as she nodded.

The car was peaceful as there was no other noise outside, and Lily didn't talk much. I stared out the window, looking for any signs of life, as she'd promised we were close. Even showing up at this time would look suspicious. Even worse, my mind ran wild that a cop would be sitting on the road waiting for us. I couldn't think about anything negative and pushed those thoughts aside. Then I saw a road up ahead that led to a house with lights on. The time was about ten, so it wasn't unusual, but it had to be them.

Lily was looking straight ahead at it, and I moved my hand to touch hers. Looking over with a hardened expression, she nodded.

"Okay, we need a plan. We have no money or drugs to deal with them if that is them," I said, staring straight ahead. Lily leaned over, surprised. "Are you suggesting we rob them?"

I didn't answer for a moment until I told her, "If I know who this is, then it might come to that."

She grabbed my hand, almost yanking the car left. "What the fuck does that mean, Michael?"

Annoyed, definitely due to withdrawals and the fact that a person who could have been involved in my father's death was ahead, I knew I had to lock myself into the situation. Keeping my voice calm, I told her, "If the son is there, you can keep him distracted. If the dad is there, just let me handle it. If things go sideways, say the name of our town and get behind something."

Her eyes widened.

"Lily, look at me. Can you do that? We won't survive unless you listen to me in this situation."

With a huff, she sat back in her seat and said she would do it.

With my destination in sight, I couldn't help but feel emotions I hadn't felt in over a year. I didn't recognize them, and it made me feel strange. Anxious but filled with excitement. A bit of happiness? All I could think of was how fucked up I was. Getting closer to the house, I killed the lights and told Lily we would go to the front door and she would knock. Killing the ignition, I got out as Lily did and went to my backpack. I put my revolver in the back of my waistband and my bayonet in my sweater. I deliberately made sure Lily couldn't see.

Even if she'd wanted to, all she did when she got out was stare at the house in front of us. I went over to her and looked at it. It was huge, had multiple cars parked outside, and looked like a family that came from wealth. I nudged her. "You sure this is your contact's place?"

Not facing me, she told me, "It's the best I've got."

Half-baked plans weren't my forte, but hell, I was already on the run from the police and had no home to go back to. Backing down wasn't an option.

Reaching out my hand to hers, we walked forward. The forest around us was quiet except for the owls. I wondered what could lurk in those dark woods. Something worse than a human? I was tempted to let everything go and walk straight into the forest, as if I were being controlled, but I snapped back to my senses.

"Lily, I need some painkillers. Do you have oxy or anything?"

She shook her head. "I only have Vicodin on me."

I told her that would do, and she took a couple of pills out of her jacket pocket and handed them to me. Throwing them into my mouth, I felt better knowing I'd have drugs in my system for this. My mind had to be focused.

"You know, I used to come up here a lot with Lucas. I would beg him to take me, and he would always tell me no. But you know me. I always get my way," she said, laughing.

Lucas. I did not want to remember Lucas right now, but Lily droned on.

"So Lucas was really into sports and had a nice family, but every time we would come up here, I'd watch him change just a little bit. Soon he came to me and said we could sell drugs together."

I interrupted her. "You use the same sales pitch on every boy you date?"

She got quieter. I'd hurt her feelings.

"I don't. I mean, I didn't love him like I did with you. He was a good guy, and I felt like that's what I liked about him. When I brought him into this, it started to change him. And then he." She paused. "Then he died."

She trailed off, staring out the window.

"I killed him, Michael. I bear it with me every day. He was so nice before all this. You would have liked him. And I turned him into this, and he overdosed. I'm a killer." She started to sob into her jacket.

How did I tell her I was the one who did it and it wasn't her fault? I didn't even realize how much this had affected her.

"Lily, you did nothing wrong. He started the drugs, and you know that's just what happens."

She shook her head. "You just don't get it. You didn't have to go to his parents' house and tell them what happened. You didn't have to hear them talk about their baby boy and how he would have never done this. I'm fucking scarred from it. You can't just unsee them."

I had to console her somehow. "Lil, I promise it isn't your fault, and with time it will get better. I'm here to help you too."

She nodded and placed her hand on mine. "I just hope he's up in heaven watching me right now confess, so he knows I'm sorry I killed him."

I gritted my teeth. "He probably is."

Silence ensued as we walked along the road to the house. I was anxious and grinding my teeth while Lily silently cried a bit more over Lucas. Would I ever be able to tell her? I could lift the burden off her shoulders, but she would hate me forever for it. I decided there wasn't time for that and kept on moving.

"Do you see all the stars? Look at the constellations and how beautiful they are," Lily said as we walked. She was right. As I looked up, there were so many stars I could sit here the whole night and count them. Oh, to be a star and shine bright and watch over the entire world. "They are wonderful," was all I could utter as my eyes were glued to the sky. A star shot across at lightning speed and was gone. Lily commented on it, having seen it too.

"That shooting star reminds me of a human's life. Over in the blink of an eye, but so very beautiful."

The Last Time

With the house looming over us, Lily and I were dwarfed in comparison. I'd been listening for any human activity the whole way here but had failed to hear anything. My chest constricted standing in the presence of this enormous house in front of me. The night sky shone down, illuminating everything around us. I looked over at Lily, who side-eyed me and finally broke down.

"Mikey, I'm in over my head. I have been from the beginning. This is madness. We can leave and figure something out."

I shook my head no. "Please," she pleaded, and I looked at her with my dead eyes, giving the door two knocks.

The wait for someone to answer felt like it lasted millennia. So many thoughts flooded my brain about who would respond. What would this person look like? Would this Lillan guy have a wife who answered? So many random thoughts ran through me like shocks hitting all at once.

Not knowing how long I'd spaced out, I finally heard someone squeak the door open. I was looking at a pair of brown eyes that looked at me and then at Lily to my right.

"What do you need at this time?" the eyes asked.

Lily spoke out. "It's me, Lily. We're here to buy, you know what."

Silence ensued while the eyes thought this over.

"The last guy you came with looked a bit different, you know?" the voice said as the door opened and I saw a boy who looked about our age.

He had brown hair to match his eyes and was about my height. Assessing him, I thought there was a reasonable chance I could take him. Lily, now seeing him fully, said, "I'm not with him anymore. This is my friend, and he wants to buy more than we ever bought in the past."

Sensing this was my cue, I had to take control of the situation. "Nice to meet you. I'm Davis. I want to buy as much as you have on you, and I've got no limit to my money."

The brown-haired boy still stood at the door with his arm glued to the handle. "Do you think I'm a fool? How do I know you're not trying to set me up?"

I pulled out my pitiful remaining Xanax from my wallet and showed him a couple hundred dollars. "I don't want to waste any time. I'm here to buy."

He changed his tone and told me to come in. "My name's Rustin. I have most of the stuff in the basement, but I'd need my dad to unlock it."

Gathering info from this, something didn't add up. "Why do you have a basement if you live on the West Coast?"

Rustin shrugged. "You'd have to ask my dad."

This weird interaction made me feel uneasy, but I let it go. Lily grabbed Rustin and told him everything we wanted. I hadn't told her to do this, but I was glad, since I still didn't know much about opiates.

The whole house was sketching me the fuck out. I knew Lily wouldn't be of much help, so I sat around while Rustin talked about some bullshit I tuned out. Nothing added up here. This house was too nice, and I had never heard of it. The pictures on the wall never showed Rustin, but an older man with all his friends. Was he renting this house? I felt dread rising in me. This was not a spot I wanted to be in.

I asked Rustin about it, to which he replied, "Oh, my dad has a lot of connections through Astorium and loves to take pictures with them."

I nodded. "So your dad is pretty popular, I take it? Why have I never heard of him?"

Lily shot me a look. I rolled my eyes at her.

Rustin looked over at me with contempt. "Because he's a fucking drug dealer. Did your dad do drugs? No? Then why would my dad know him?"

I wanted to knock this kid's teeth out for mentioning my father, but I finally heard someone upstairs.

Rustin spoke to me again. "Say, what does your dad do, if you're judging mine?"

There wasn't a need to lie here. "My dad shot himself. He's dead. He doesn't do much of anything anymore, I suppose."

I heard someone coming down the stairs, and Rustin's face was one of confusion. I didn't care. This needed to be done, and Lily and I needed to get out of here. I could think these scenarios over in my head later.

Rustin started to walk towards the back of his house. "Just stay here. I'll go get my dad, and we can work out a deal."

He jogged upstairs and left Lily and me alone. Turning to her, I whispered, "Keep him occupied. Once you see the goods, just say something I'd understand, and I'll take over."

Looking zoned out, she sadly nodded. I grabbed her. "Look, I need you more than ever right now. Please, please, put on a smile."

I sensed I might have been putting too much on her, but she told me, "Fine. Just for now. Everything better work out."

I gave her a thumbs-up and told her it would.

Hearing two people talking and coming down the stairs, I braced myself and felt my revolver at my waist. From what I knew, no one else was in this house, which was lucky. Maybe luck was on my side for once. My stomach turned, wondering what was in store, and I knew this had to go right. Just stick to the plan and let it work out.

The two came over to us. I clocked the older one at around six feet tall and bigger than me. Taking care of him would be a task. I'd have to use whatever social engineering I had left. The man spoke up. "Rustin told me you've bought before and you're looking to buy ten grand of pills and heroin?"

Ten grand. What the fuck was Lily thinking? I'd have to have a briefcase of money to make that believable. I remembered my dad telling me once, "Confidence is key. If people think you fit in, you will."

Using this, I stepped up. "Yes. I moved on from selling benzodiazepines since most people want uppers now, and my friend here said you guys had the best in stock."

He looked me over and shrugged. "Alright. Inventory's downstairs. Follow me."

I watched him and Rustin walk downstairs. I followed, grabbing Lily's hand and helping her down, as she didn't seem fully present.

"Here's where I keep most of the heroin I get. All the oxy, Vicodin, and percs are down here," the man said. I looked at the closet he'd opened, and it almost blinded me. The amount of drugs was staggering. Figuring out the price shouldn't be too hard if I asked. I moved around pretending to inspect for details and stepped back with my hands behind me.

"How much to buy all of this?" I told him. The man laughed. "Buy all of this? Kid, you'd need at least twenty grand, and unless you have a magic source of money, I don't see twenty grand here."

I explained quickly. "I have cash on me. The rest is in my car. If you want to help me get this all loaded into bags."

Looking at me, I don't think he could tell if I was serious. "I'm good for it. You can trust me. My friend has been buying off you for months."

Lily, finally snapping back, must have realized I needed her. "He's right. I've been buying with Rustin for months."

The man looked over to Rustin to ask if this was true, to which Rustin replied, "She's been here a lot. I can't deny that. But it was with a different guy."

His father thought this over and looked at me. "My son told me your name is Davis."

I didn't understand if this was a question or a statement. I looked up, carelessly motioning with my hand. "Yeah, that's my name."

I watched as he took this in and seemed to be thinking of something. I sensed things could get bad at an instant's notice. He'd realized something. I tried to de-escalate. "You never told me your name. It's only right if we both know ours if we're doing such a big deal."

The man nodded. "You're right. My name is Paul."

I began to respond with something polite, but he kept going. "But you lied about your name."

I pointed towards myself without speaking, raising my eyebrows.

"I know you. You're Christopher's kid."

I felt my brain zap and clutched my right hand with my left. That was the first time I'd heard his name said in so long.

"I noticed it. You're the spitting image of your father. Funny thing, he was a user and now you're a dealer."

Still gripping my right hand, I spoke back. "Let's just get the deal done. My father is long dead."

"He owed too much money. I suppose he shouldn't have kept buying opiates. Nice guy, your father. It hurt me when I realized they were going after him."

I moved back slowly to where Lily was stationed with Rustin. As I walked, I spoke in a soothing voice. "After him?"

Paul shook his head. "He bought off me and my people all the time. Said his home life was bad. Lost a lot of money on drugs and didn't have the money to pay it back. Last time he left this house, he told me he'd pay it back."

Paul moved to close the closet. "Since you're his son, you have to pay his debts. Everything here is forty grand."

"I can settle my father's debts. That's fine," I said as my mind warped around and my hand shook with anger. I was lined up with his son now and had my hand in my sweater, ready to pull the bayonet from its sheath.

"However, that was my father's debt. Why should I answer for his sins?" I asked to play with him. Paul was beginning to put a lock on the closet. Hesitation is death. I pulled the knife from the sheath and put it to Rustin's neck. Rustin cried out, and his father turned around. I stared at him. "Put everything you have in bags, or I'll make the debt my father owed you even bigger."

I sliced through some of the skin on Rustin's throat. Lily watched and smartly backed away towards the wall. Paul, not seeming fazed, opened the closet back up and turned towards me with a gun in hand.

"I never thought a teenager would try to rob me, but here we are. Stupid, just like your father."

I held Rustin's face in front of mine as best I could to block any shot he fired at me. His gun looked like a Glock, and I felt my pulse rise. This was life or death, and I had to be in control.

"Last chance, Paul. Ten seconds before I cut his throat."

Paul laughed. "You have no idea who you're dealing with here. As soon as you do that, your little girlfriend is dead."

From my point of view, I hadn't seen his gun move, and now it was aimed right at Lily, who was in the corner. I couldn't lose Lily, and I couldn't lose the drugs. Where was the winning option? Lily spoke to me. "Astorium." As she said the word, she sprinted towards a table and dove behind it. Shots rang out all around my right side, and as they did, I slit Rustin's throat as hard as I could, feeling the bone. Blood sprayed everywhere in front of me, and I held his body in front of me with one hand. Paul screamed something, but my eardrums had been blown out by the shots, and I couldn't hear it. I felt it, though, as the rounds he fired went through his son and skimmed my right arm. I dropped to the ground and crawled over to a table, pulled out my .22, and cocked it.

My hands were covered in blood, my body felt like I'd been hit with hammers everywhere, and my eyes couldn't focus. I felt fear as I pictured Paul coming up behind me and putting one in my head, and everything going black. Crawling around, smoke was coming from everywhere, and I heard someone scream. Knowing it had to be Lily, I peeked out in that direction, aiming my revolver in front of me.

Everything seemed covered in smoke as I caught a glimpse of two people fighting. It looked like Paul was on top of her, so I fired every round I had at him. More screams pierced my ears as the smoke diluted my senses. I got up and went over to look at Paul, who had rolled off of Lily and been shot a good number of times. I looked at Lily, then away. Paul's gun was to the left, and I went over and picked it up.

Standing next to him, I crouched down and put it to his head. "This one's for my father."

The shot rang out, and blood covered me. "This one's for Lily," I said as I shot again. At that point, I couldn't hear anything but knew what needed to be done. I looked towards Lily and then the closet. I dashed towards it, grabbing bags of every drug and putting them in one big bag. I cleaned out the whole inventory in a mad rage and dragged it all back to Lily.

"Help. Me," she mumbled. There was so much blood on her that I couldn't tell the extent of her injuries.

"I'll get you out of here. We got what we came for," I said, putting my bloody hand in hers. The smoke had gotten worse, and a fire had started. Soon, the police and firetrucks would be here. There was no way I could get Lily and the drugs to the car at the same time.

Lily reached out her hand to me. "I told you, I was in over my head, Mikey."

Her hand reached up to cup my cheek, and I stared at her as the sprinklers and fire destroyed my nostrils with a bloody metallic tang. "Michael." Her voice was different now. Not the Lily who'd called me Mikey all my life. "You don't need to run anymore." Her hand fell as her eyes went glossy. I can save her. I can save her. I can save her.

I knew I needed to get out of there. My life would be engulfed in flames. Hesitation is death. I grabbed Lily gently and picked her up.

"Just close your eyes. I'm going to take you to the hospital," I told her. I wasn't sure if she could hear me from all the gunshots, but reassuring her made me believe in myself. I carried her out of the house and walked fast towards the car.

Getting to the car, I laid her against it and unlocked the back doors. Picking her up again, I laid her down on the back seat. "I'll be back in three minutes."

She didn't respond. I started to sprint as fast as I could to the front door of the house. I could hear sirens off in the distance and knew I wasn't going to make it. Failure.

"I will not be a failure," I screamed at myself. I kept running and swooped into the front door. Running to the basement, I grabbed the bag of drugs and took them upstairs towards the front. My whole body wanted to collapse, but I had to keep going. No matter what, this wasn't how it was going to end for me or her. Running back, I could see the lights as the whole back of the house had begun to burn. It didn't matter. Both of them were dead. They'd just be chasing some random murderer. And yeah, someone who was on house arrest had just left a couple of hours ago and this happened. I was fucked if they caught me.

I got to the car and turned it on, throwing it into drive as fast as I could, and went north. I drove north, watching the lights get closer and closer and the blaze get bigger and bigger. What destruction had I caused over some pills? That wasn't even counting the two people I'd just killed. In my mind, it was self-defense, but I doubted a judge would see it that way.

My brain couldn't register what was going on as I drove. I looked around me and saw tree after tree, a repeating cycle of clones. That was what humans were. The same pest, always multiplying. There was no order to things. Order would have saved the girl I loved. Now she was sitting in the back of my car. Another tree. Another gravestone.

Another body to be buried. I smashed my hands into the steering wheel over and over. Why couldn't I think? Why couldn't I save her? I loved her and had failed her. I ran through what happened again. I could have shot him first. I could have killed Rustin and waited for his dad to come down and killed him too. Fuck. Why did it always involve killing to save her? I should have never gone there in the first place. Fucking idiot.

I slammed the car into park, hearing the metal screech as if it was mirroring my anger. My head rested on the steering wheel as I cried. I couldn't stop the tears from flowing. Why did it have to be her? Why couldn't it have been me? I loved her so much. She was the only person to take me in as a friend. The only person to help me through my father's death. The one I felt most comfortable with. The one I had laid in bed with and felt what a true free human feels like.

I was a monster. I couldn't fix this situation. It was all over. I pulled the .22 from my waist and started to cry hopelessly. I could end all this pain. All would be made right in the world if I was gone. I would never see Lily again. Wherever I was going, it certainly wasn't to heaven where Lily lay. I didn't know what to do.

Putting the metal to the side of my head, I stared outside my windshield. Nobody would find me here for a while. It would be a good resting place. "I'm sorry, Lily," I told her. I couldn't look into the backseat. I didn't want to accept reality. She could just be resting.

I was done with life. I didn't want anything from it, and it didn't want anything from me. I wasn't scared in that moment. I think I remembered watching a show about how people are always scared in their last moments. They weren't me. I had conviction.

I whispered I'm sorry one more time to Lily and pulled the trigger.

I blinked as I heard the click.

I was still here.

I had used all the bullets when I shot Rustin's father.

I couldn't even kill myself.

I threw the gun out the right window, smashing it to bits, and put the car in drive.

Fuck you, life.

I kept driving for so long, still covered in blood, until I found a lake, to which I pulled off the road. I got out and opened the doors. Seeing Lily like this made me go numb. Using the drugs I'd taken for good, I wrapped up her arm and gave her what I could, then poured painkillers down her throat. I then carried her to the lake, our blood falling from us like a waterfall.

I ripped my clothes off to my boxers and went into the water. I grabbed them all, dove as far as I could to the bottom, and put a rock over them. Doing this almost resulted in me drowning, as I realized when I pushed off from the bottom that I had no energy. Getting to the surface, I coughed up blood and water.

Forever looking down at Lily was the moon, which illuminated her. She didn't move, and I went over to strip her of her bloody clothes. Once they were off, I carried her to the water where the blood washed off her, as if to cleanse all her sins. Her body had been littered with bullet holes. I think I'd known this since I first saw her after I shot Paul, but I still believed she would be okay.

Going back to the lake's edge, I lay her on the grass and grasped her cheek.

"Lily. Lily. Can you wake up? We made it. We're going to be okay," I said as I hovered over her still body. I began to shake her. "Lily, please, please, please wake up now. Tell me I'm an idiot. Tell me you need my help. Talk to me, please."

I held out my hand as I looked up at the stars. A light rain had started to fall, and the moon reflected off the lake right to me. I fell back and stared at her. My eyes felt watery, and I began to weep. Not for any of my previous actions tonight. Just for Lily. The girl I'd grown up with. The girl I'd loved. The girl I would do anything for.

"I'm sorry, Lily. I couldn't save you."

I leaned down and pressed my forehead to hers. Her skin was cold, and the rain fell between us like it was trying to separate what was already gone. I whispered the words I had told her before.

"It's always been you."

She looked so beautiful in my mind, lying there in the rain in front of the lake. A part of me hoped she was with the stars, looking down on me and telling me everything was going to be okay. I knew when I got up, my life was over, and everything would be worse. I would have no purpose to live. I looked at her one last time for a while, saying goodbye to both of our lives.

Destruction

I ripped out the fabric of the front and back seats of my car as best I could. Using a knife wasn't the handiest thing, but it was all I could think of. When I held it in my right hand, I put my left arm across it. I wanted to feel pain. I wanted to die. The blood seeped off my hand and splattered onto the dirt road.

Popping my trunk, I put on new clothes and combed my hair, which was an utter mess from the water. I hauled the drug bag to the trunk, put it in, and went back to the driver's seat. I sat there with the car off. I began to bang my fists against the wheel over and over. There was no way out of this. What did I even do at this point? Staring out my window, I saw a deer pass by. It was such a beautiful creature that the mere sight of it calmed me down. If there were deer, I must be close to northern Washington.

I was almost out of gas and needed to find a place to fill up to continue my journey. I could hit the road right now, but the thought of cops and my wanted poster being everywhere terrified me. I'd left my gun in the house, which they'd track to me, and the same with my bayonet. They would find Lily's body today. I was sure they were mounting a search to find me when the sun came up.

Like a king in check, my only move was forward. I put it into drive and went down the road looking for a station. I saw a sign and looked over to the passenger seat to tell Lily there was a gas station ahead, but then I realized I was alone. Lily was lying dead in the grass while I drove on.

Getting closer to the gas station, the paranoia of cops was hitting me so hard, along with the Xanax withdrawals, that I pulled over and popped the trunk. I'd only done heroin a couple of times, but this was the first time I'd willingly gone to it out of need. I found a vein, pushed the needle in, and felt on top of the world.

Nothing bad had occurred. I was in heaven now. I tried to focus on the road and sloppily pulled into pump three. Getting out of the car, I fell and scraped my knee, but there was no pain. I'd overdone the dosage by a fuckton and needed to get this car filled up. I didn't want to use hundred-dollar bills since cashiers always gave funny looks when you paid with them, so I was glad to see I had a couple of twenties.

I don't remember much of going inside, but I met a small man whom I told I was filling up on pump three, keep the change, and focused on how to walk out. One foot at a time. I remember filling up the car and hitting the limit. I had no care in the world. It was as if everything bad had turned for the better.

Getting into my car to get away, I pulled out and saw a town sign that said five miles. If I focused hard enough, I could make it to a hotel, plus it was still dark, which meant nobody, I hoped, would be on the road. Going forward, the minutes went by, and I arrived in a town called Rupi, which had a hotel directly upon arrival.

I parked my car as far away as I could from the building in the parking lot to avoid suspicion and went to the front office. Trying the doors proved useless, so I rang the doorbell. A woman appeared and let me in. I asked her for three nights, to which I think she thought I was flirting. I pulled out two hundred from my wallet and gave it to her. I told her I might need to stay longer, and this would cover it. Looking at her, she couldn't have been much older than me. She asked what my name was, and I almost said Michael, but switched it up in my hazardous state just in time to say "Jackson." I thought it funny that my brain thought of Michael Jackson when coming up with an alias and started to laugh, which startled her, but she began to laugh with me.

After this, she got the room keys and led me down the hall. I thanked her and opened my door, where I immediately went into the shower. I scrubbed at all the wounds that were still a bit bloody, but nothing seemed to come off. The more I tried to clean, the more I bled. I gave up and almost died getting out of the shower. I put a towel around me, went straight to bed, and under the covers. I took one last look at my room and saw it had a small window and a door that led to the parking lot. I thought this convenient, and then I slipped into my heroin dreams.

. . .

I don't know how long I was out, but when I got up, the window shone bright, and I ran to the bathroom to throw up everything in my body. I lay against the wall naked and shaking. I hugged myself as I heard voices and people outside. I thought for sure someone would bust into my room, and I stared at the door, but minutes passed and nothing happened as the voices faded on and off.

I held out my hands and watched them shake. I was done. There was no more forward for me. Crawling towards my bed, I got to my bag and pulled out clothes, putting them on while sprawled on the floor. I took a quarter of a Xanax from the bag, which I'd cut earlier, and popped as many painkillers as I could. Get up. My body wouldn't react to my mind. I tried to stand, but nothing worked. I was a broken, empty shell of a human being.

Assessing the situation from where I lay, I concluded that I didn't have much time left before I was arrested or shot. That was never how I'd dreamed of dying or ending my life. This encouraged my body to move as I staggered to the wall next to me. I was going to take Lily to the beach. I must be close. Making sure I had my keys, I wobbled out of the room to the front desk, where I saw the girl from earlier. She told me good afternoon.

I'd thought it was morning, so this came as a surprise, and when I asked the time, she told me it was two in the afternoon. I didn't have much time left. I could picture a clock in my mind, the remaining time rapidly dropping. Tick. Tick. Tick. Thanking her, I asked if there was a beach nearby.

"Of course. Rupi Beach. It's just five minutes northwest of here," she told me as if this were common knowledge. I nodded and thanked her.

Getting to my car, all I could think about was the endless freedom the beach had to offer. I wished I could have been a wave, flowing up and down all day in the cool air. Being born as a human was the biggest mistake God had made for me. Whatever I touched was destroyed, and whatever I built was ruined. I tried to shake off tears but still felt my eyes get watery.

As I drove through town, it wasn't hard to find. On the main road, a huge sign said Rupi Beach, 1.5 miles, with an arrow to the left. I almost turned, but it hit me that I hadn't eaten or drank anything in over a day. I was overcome with hunger that gnawed at my very existence. I parked my car on the side of the road and headed to the local diner.

I ordered the usual chicken tenders with fries when the waitress came over. I decided on water instead of soda because I felt dehydrated. While I ate, I looked at my food and was overcome with sadness, as there was supposed to be a person sitting across from me. If she were here right now, she'd be eating all my fries like she always did. I looked up, expecting to see her, but only saw a leather booth staring back at me.

She had never deserved this. I could only imagine what her mother felt, to lose her child. Katrina probably didn't even know Lily was dead yet. She was probably thinking about how Lily acted every other time she'd run off. "She'll be back later," I could imagine her saying to me. I had ruined her life in the process of what? What a fucking idiot I was.

I left a twenty on the table and went back to my car. I glanced around the town to see that it was empty. It reminded me of a ghost town, or a town you'd see in your dreams. No one was outside, and nobody was on the road. This was perfectly fine with me. I'd always imagined living on the earth by myself. Nobody to bother me.

Starting towards the beach, I took the turns slowly and watched all the scenery around me. Trees that almost looked like a forest surrounded the road, making it impossible to believe this led to a beach, let alone an ocean. Everything started to blend in, and my mind went back to seeing Lily lying in the grass surrounded by the lake and trees. I pleaded with my mind to stop thinking about it, but it was etched there. A haunting image I could never forget, which I had ultimately caused.

Going around loops and turns, my mind was elsewhere. What did I have left to do? I would run out of money soon, but I had drugs, just nobody to sell them to. I could go back to Nicole or call her, but I was sure they'd tapped her phone lines. It felt like all roads led to my despair, and nothing would go right for me. Maybe it was what I deserved. All the terrible things I'd done.

As I reached the end, I saw a small parking lot and the beach. Parking my car and getting out, I started the long walk over to the water, which was hitting the rocks. In my head, I only felt bad about what had happened to Lily, yet I'd killed other people too. I knew it was wrong, but for some stupid reason, I couldn't find any reason to mourn them. I'd disliked them, and they'd meant nothing to me. They were obstacles in my path and had to be dealt with. I assumed my soul was fucked, as I couldn't feel much emotion for any of them. All I wanted was to be here with Lily.

The beach was as beautiful and quiet as ever. The sky was cloudy, and high rocks would allow you to climb and see more of the ocean. To my right, I saw cliffs that rose high above, with eagles flying around. If only you had been here to see this. In another life, I'm holding her hand as we watch the water creep up to us and fall back as if it's a game, but I stood here alone in solace, regretting my actions that brought me here.

I dropped to the ground and sat watching the waves. Taking some pills from my pocket, I swallowed as many as I could and sat there until I could feel pure bliss. Lily's voice rang out to me as I looked forward, and I could see our memories together. Walking to school, chasing each other around town. In my mind, she was still here. In a brief moment, I was startled as an orange cat ran over me.

Sure that I'd taken too many pills, I focused on it and saw a man following not too far behind who gave me a wave, which I returned. I couldn't tell if any of this was real or not, and my heart started to race, making me itch for a Xanax. Before I could get to my wallet, the man spoke out. "Sorry. She never sees anyone here, so she must have been interested in you."

I stared at the man and then directed my eyes towards the cat, who had plopped down in the sand, staring at me with heavy green eyes. I waved my hand to tell him it was all right.

"We don't see people here very often, so I bring this little one out here all the time. She thinks it's her litter-box heaven," the man said with a hefty laugh.

I couldn't get a read on him, but I assumed he was harmless and not a police officer, so I sat in silence. The man, however, kept talking. "After my wife passed, I had no one until this little one showed up on my doorstep." He gave her a scratch on the ear as he said this.

I finally spoke back. "I'm sorry to hear that."

The man shifted his gaze from me to the ocean in front of us. "It's all right, son. You just have to remember never to lose hope. Some happiness will come your way."

I picked up sand and let it fall through my fingertips. "I don't think that applies to everyone."

The cat came over as I kept picking up sand and letting it fall. It tried to claw at it like a game, which gave me a slight amusement.

"Sounds like you're talking about yourself there, son. I've been where you are. It doesn't last forever, even when you want it to. You have to take it one day at a time, and something good will come your way," the man said. I didn't mind him talking to me, and the genuine sound in his voice made me feel a bit better inside, but I knew it was all for naught. I couldn't exactly tell him my love was dead and I'd killed other people. No good was ever coming my way, and I didn't deserve it.

The cat started to walk back to its owner as he called it. "I hope you find what you're looking for. This place out here is beautiful. Stay long enough and it might come to you," he said as he started to walk away. He gave me a final wave, and I meekly waved back. What was I looking for at this point? I knew the answer, and it wasn't anything good. I lay back in the sand watching the clouds above me. I loved how if you stared at them closely enough, you could see how fast they moved. I envied them, to be a cloud, just floating along with the wind. I envied everything that wasn't me.

Satisfied with what I'd seen, I went over to the water to touch it as it came to me. How badly I wanted to walk out as far as I could and be washed out to sea. For nobody to ever find my body. There wasn't any way I was going to end up in a cell. I would face my punishment for my wrongdoings in the afterlife, not here, where everything I loved was dead.

I started to trek back to the car and spotted a payphone near the entrance of the lot. Why not give her a call? It couldn't hurt to gain any information. Opening my wallet, I saw the zipper and got a couple of quarters out. I stood there with a blank face, unsure of what to do next, but I needed something. Anything to fill what I felt right now. Just hearing her talk to me might bring me back in some way.

I pushed the coins into the slot and dialed her number while the sky above me started to sprinkle. The payphone had a tiny structure over it, so I was able to slide into it while I heard the phone dial.

"Hello?" is what I heard when the dial stopped. I was frozen. What could I possibly say to her? I was tired of lying. If I got caught because of this, so fucking be it. "Hey, Nicole. It's me," I responded in the casual voice she was used to.

"Mikey?" She paused for a moment. "Michael, I've been so worried about you. The police came to me asking about you, and I heard you went to jail, and a lot of it was my fault. I'm sorry, it's..." I cut her off, as I didn't want to talk about any of that. "That doesn't matter to me, Nicole.

Listen, I know this is on a recorded line, I'm sure of it, but it's not your fault about the Xanax. They were all mine, and I hid them at your house without you knowing."

The least I could do was get her off the hook with the law by placing all the blame on me. She didn't understand why I was saying that, as I could tell in her tone. She sounded like she wanted to cry as she spoke. "Why are you saying all of this? Just come home. We have the whole summer, and we have our future to plan out."

Hearing her say those words felt like a lifetime ago. I responded. "I have no home anymore. I want to come and find you, but I simply can't. Please don't hate me forever. You gave me so many memories, and you're going to go on and live your best life."

The rain had started to come down, and I could barely hear her, but all I could think about were tears.

"I'm glad we met, Nicole. I am."

I set the phone down on the hook and rushed to my car, where I sat in the passenger seat watching the rain smother my window. I couldn't see anything except the glistening of my eyes filling with the remainder of the tears I had left. All the times I'd had with her soared through my mind. If I went back for her and somehow miraculously started a life with her, she would meet the same fate as Lily. I was a cancer to everything I touched. I felt as if I could walk outside and touch a flower and watch it wither up and die. She had her life, and I couldn't ruin it. I couldn't keep making mistakes and hating myself anymore. I was too tired of it. Looking in my mirrors, I tried to see the beach, but all I saw was water covering it, and as time passed, the storm grew considerably darker.

I went into the backseat and pulled out some sweatshirts to make a headrest and blankets. Driving out of this would end in a wreck, which would end my life. Reaching for my backpack, I took a water bottle and some oxys, popping them into my mouth and finishing the water. Lying down to the sound of rain all around me, I was surrounded, trapped in nature's mercy.

Time

My dreams were ill-begotten and took me back to places I'd never wanted to see. Sitting in a chair watching my therapist talk to me and ask me questions after my father died. Trying out new medications every month to see if anything would help my anxiety and depression. In my dreams, I felt as if I were watching the past and not doing anything else. My time had passed, and this was the result I'd gotten.

The sun woke me as it beamed into the car. I got up quietly to check the windows, but nobody was in the parking lot. The pills had worn off, and I took more with some of the remaining Xanax and decided to get moving. Strangely, my brain couldn't process any thoughts, and I found myself on the road back to Astorium.

The highway stretched out in front of me and I drove without thinking. My hands were on the wheel but I wasn't really driving. My body was doing it for me while my brain was somewhere else entirely.

I looked over at the passenger seat and Lily was sitting there. She was looking out the window with her hair blowing even though the windows were closed. I opened my mouth to tell her we were almost home and then she was gone. Just an empty seat with a stain on it that I didn't want to think about.

I turned the radio on because the silence was making me hear things. Every song sounded like it was written about me. I changed the station and the next one was worse. I turned it off and drove in the silence again.

A sign came up on the right for a hospital. My foot hovered over the brake. I thought about my mom in whatever facility they'd taken her to, hundreds of miles away. I could turn around right now and drive south until I found her. I could walk in and just hold her and let her hold me and be a kid again for five minutes.

I kept driving. I watched the sign disappear in my rearview mirror and that was that.

Every set of headlights behind me was a cop. I was sure of it. I changed lanes and slowed down and watched them pass me every single time. Just trucks and families and people going somewhere that wasn't a jail cell. My hands were gripping the wheel so hard my knuckles were white and I couldn't get them to relax.

I passed a sign that said Astorium, 40 miles. Forty miles between me and everything I had destroyed. My brain told me to keep driving north and never stop. My hands turned the wheel south. I was going back. I didn't know why. I didn't have a reason. But the town was pulling me in like it always had, like it would never let me go.

As I drove, I became more paranoid and nauseated thinking of what was waiting for me. For once in my life, I didn't have a plan. My mother was far away, and everyone I knew was dead, and the one friend I had, I'd let go of. I drove for hours just watching what was in front of me. Nothing mattered anymore.

When I got into town, I was surprised at the lack of police presence. I drove straight to my house and decided that if a cop were there, I'd make my stand, as I didn't have anything to live for. However, I pulled into the driveway and was greeted with utter silence. It spooked the fuck out of me. I opened the garage door and then closed it. Grabbing my stuff from the car, I opened the door, expecting to see police everywhere with grins ready to take me in, but saw nothing.

Wondering what was going on, I hunkered up in my room, which was entirely cleaned out, and set my stuff down. My brain wanted to think about all of this, but I was so tired of living and craving a high that I pulled some heroin out of the stash and tied up my arm. I sat there with my mouth hanging open, staring at my open door, and began to laugh. Nothing felt real, and everything felt amazing. Nobody was coming to get me. My mind was free. I danced around my empty room to music I thought was playing all around me before collapsing onto my bed.

Grabbing my backpack, I took out a sweater and some other clothes and laid them on the bed before heading to the shower. The hot water felt like heaven, and I found myself standing in the same place for minutes, letting the water flow off me without even noticing time flying by.

Cleaning myself up the best I could, I looked in the mirror and saw how good I looked. My pupils were huge, which made me crack a smile, and I headed back to my room to get dressed. After putting everything on, I couldn't think of what to do, so I picked up the pills I had and started imagining targets on the wall and throwing them. They bounced all around my room until I hit my dresser and saw a note sticking out. It was the one Lily had left me.

Rereading the note, it sounded like Nicole's voice, not Lily. It was too careful. I crashed back onto my bed, chucking more pills at my wall before deciding I was going to ask her about it. I couldn't think of anything that could go wrong, and my body felt so good, something I hadn't felt in ages.

I decided not to drive and take in the scenery of my town. As I walked, I found myself stumbling a couple of times and looking all around me to see if anyone had seen. I wanted to feel like this forever, I thought, over and over. When I got closer to her house, I knew knocking on the door would have been stupid, and luckily, she lived on the first floor.

I felt delusions all around. I saw memories of us walking through her front door and leaving, laughing together in the bedroom, and being together forever. My body was breaking down with all the drugs I'd been taking, and I was starting to see how terrible it was. The pain was too immense, and I gave into the hellish world as I reached for more pills in my pocket and took them.

At her window, I gave a two-finger knock and waited. The blinds were opened a crack and then shut. The window was slid open as I heard her speak. "Why are you here? I told you on the phone..."

I spoke up to cut her off. "I know, Nicole. I know. I have nothing left. I came back to see if I could feel anything. I see delusions all around me, and my past haunts me. I'm going to hell, and there is no road off."

Nicole opened the blinds and waved at me to come in while putting her other finger in a hush motion. Standing in her room brought so many memories that I couldn't deal with.

"We should have stayed in this room. Together and forever," I said aloud, staring at her bed as if imagining an alternate timeline. Nicole frowned as she sat down. She had something on her mind, and I gave her a glance of annoyance.

"The police have come by asking for you multiple times," she said, glancing down.

I swayed around the room. "The police have always had a grudge against me. They didn't help with my father and sent my mother to the nuthouse."

Nicole was nodding, taking all of this in, looking sad. "They said you were with Lily."

Lily. There was no point in lying, and any more would make my eternal punishment worse. I could imagine myself being beaten for every lie I'd ever said to someone who cared about me.

"I was taking Lily out of state because she needed my help."

Nicole looked me straight in the eyes now. "With what?"

I didn't want to talk about Lily. I could see her fucking body rotting in the grass. Lily. Lily. Lily.

"It doesn't matter anymore. She's gone," I said to her eyes. She looked shocked and asked me the question I dreaded. "Where has she gone, Mikey?"

I regretted coming here. All there were was bad memories and interrogations. I had nobody, and Nicole would always hate me. Failure.

"She's in a better place," I said firmly. Nicole put a hand over her mouth, and we didn't talk for a few minutes. Finally, the silence was broken when she asked, "Why are you here? Be honest for once in your life, Mikey. I'm begging you."

I looked towards the window and watched as I climbed out of it, but looked back at her.

"I'm here to apologize to you for everything I've done. You're the last person in my life I have, and I want you to know I'm sorry."

She stared at me, trying to read my expression and thoughts, and said nothing. I walked to her window with a smile. "Maybe I'll see you around in the future? I'll try to make up for everything I've done."

Nicole stared at me for a long time. Then she said something that hurt me.

"I know you're not coming back, Michael."

I opened my mouth to lie, but nothing came out. She shook her head before I could try.

"I've known for a while. I'm not stupid. I just wanted to pretend a little longer."

I didn't deserve her. I never had. "Nicole, I…"

"Don't. Just go do what you need to do." Her eyes were wet, but her voice was steady. "I loved you. That part was real."

I looked at her one last time. "That part was real for me too."

With that, I walked to my car with my hoodie up to visit my mom. She was far away, but I had to reach her before I was gone. Driving through town, the police drove straight forward, not turning onto my street. Not knowing what this meant, I put my car in drive and went to the end of the street, where I could see Lily's house. There was one last thing I had to do. I turned off the car and walked to Lily's house with my hand clutching the pills in my pocket and the pills wrapping around my heart.

I Am

Katrina deserved closure for the girl she had raised and cared for. The girl whose life I had ruined with drugs. The girl I'd gotten killed. I promise I'll suffer for it, Lily. I knocked on the door, high out of my mind, and was shocked at how fast it was answered. Katrina stood in front of me in disarray. "Where is she? Where is my girl?"

I tried to take a step forward, but was interrupted. "If you step one foot closer, I'll call the police. I know what you've done."

The look she had on her face broke my heart. Katrina had been a second mother to me and had always been a kind soul, and now all I saw was a horrified look. I had truly become a monster beyond saving. I stood my ground.

"Lily passed away. It's my fault. Lord knows I loved her." That was the best I could say.

The scream Katrina let out was gut-wrenching and made me feel pain I didn't think was possible at this stage in my drug usage.

"I loved her. I loved her too much, so I always wanted to protect her. When it came to it, I realized it wasn't my role. I'm sorry, Katrina."

She had lost all focus on the world and stared off into the distance. Still staring at the ground, she spoke up. "I guess we both lost the ones we cared about."

Was she talking about Lily or my father? I looked towards her. "I've already lost everyone I cared about. I came here to apologize and then find my mom to apologize to her."

Her lifeless eyes still hadn't moved. "I was supposed to tell you. Your mother hung herself with bedsheets."

Katrina said this to me with a dead stare.

"My mother?" I uttered. She nodded and handed me a card that read a number on it. "When I saw you walking towards the house, I dreaded how I would tell you about it. But you've one-upped me."

My mother. My mother. My mother. The cop had told me where they were taking her, and I needed to call them. I read the card. The phone number was for Laces Mental Health Facility, as it was written at the bottom. Katrina was lying. It was revenge. Running away, I got into my car and sped home. I grabbed my pills and took more and more as I flipped the card between my fingers. Not knowing what to do in this situation, my body did its usual thing. I took them until I was almost looking at an empty bottle.

I let my body relax against the bed as I started to hyperventilate. The uppers with the downers made my body shake, and I couldn't hear my thoughts. I flexed my right hand to see if I was still in control. My mother. I'd left my flip phone in my drawer and went to get it. I almost fell out of bed trying to reach it. I eventually slid it open and grabbed it.

Huddling with no blankets in bed, I was against the wall, and I flipped open the phone, dialed the number, and put it to my ear. I waited as I heard the rings, and the eternity of rings flipped through my head, spiraled as if I could see them in front of me. I thought I was dying. "Laces Mental Health Facility," was all I heard from my phone, which was shaking violently in my hand. "Rachel Ren," I whispered, watching lights dance in front of me. The person on the other end wasn't sure what I meant and asked what I was calling about.

"I'm her son. Rachel Ren's son. I need to talk to my mother."

The woman put me on a brief hold as I started to space out. Another voice, this time a man's, came onto the line.

"I'm sorry, but Rachel passed away last week due to asphyxiation."

I didn't understand anything.

"What do you mean? What does that mean? I need to talk to her. You don't understand. I don't have the time."

The man took a deep sigh. "Your mother was found in her room with her bedsheets around her neck."

I didn't believe him. "That can't be true. She wouldn't do that. Listen, I know my fucking mother. Tell me what happened."

The man only gave vague responses. "All she left was a note that said she was going to see Chris. I can't disclose any more unless you come in person with proof."

I slammed the phone shut and threw it as hard as I could at my wall, watching it explode into a million pieces.

I went to her room. I don't know what I expected to find. The cops had cleaned it out weeks ago. There was nothing in there except the bed frame and the mattress and the smell. Her smell. That cheap perfume she wore mixed with something I couldn't name. It was the smell of my childhood and it hit me so hard I had to grab the doorframe.

I walked over to the bed and lay down on it. The same way I had when the cops took her. The same side she always slept on. I pulled the pillow to my face and breathed in as deep as I could, trying to get every last bit of her out of it. It was fading. Soon it would be gone completely and there would be nothing left of her in this house.

I thought about the photograph. The three of us at the baseball game. My dad's arm around her. Her smile. That stupid, beautiful smile that I hadn't seen in over a year. I thought about her promise to try harder. From now on, I can try harder. She had looked me in the eyes when she said that. I had believed her, even though I told myself I didn't.

I lay there staring at the ceiling the way she used to stare at it. I understood her now. I understood why she lay here all day and drank and took pills and disappeared inside herself. This ceiling was the last thing you saw before the world came back, and the world was not worth coming back to.

I laid there for hours. I took Xanax after Xanax trying to recreate how my mom felt. Is this how you imagined things would turn out, Mom? You promised me. Don't you remember? In this very place you promised your only son.

"Why me?" I yelled at the ceiling. This wasn't real. It had to be a trap for the police, hoping to catch me. My mother couldn't be dead.

I grabbed my bag and looked at my belongings. I still had heroin and oxy, but was low on oxy. I grabbed the heroin and wrapped my arm with the needle and injected it, feeling nothing but pure bliss. I didn't want to be in this haunted house anymore. With nowhere to go, I let my feet guide me out of the house and watched myself as I walked over to the school. Everything felt so good, and I could see all the people on the field I was walking towards. I saw Lily with her beautiful blonde hair and my father and mother in the stands as I stepped up to the plate.

They smiled at me, but as I got close, they would disappear one by one. I found myself in the dugout on the bench, staring at the ceiling. This is where my body had led me. I could see Lily sitting on my lap, her beautiful eyes looking up at me. Everything was cloudy and sunny, and it felt so good. "I miss you," came off her lips, and I could see the words reflected in front of me. "I miss you too," I told her. "I miss you more than you could imagine."

My body was starting to sink into the walls, and I rolled over on the bench to rest as I saw people walking towards me on the field. Which people would it be this time? I didn't know. Lily and Nicole, perhaps in an angrier mood? I wanted Nicole to forgive me deep down. I wanted to go back there and plead with her, no matter how many times she rejected me.

"What are you doing here?" an unfamiliar girlish voice said. There were two girls in front of me, and I recognized them from some corner of my brain.

"He's a drug addict. Look at him. He can't even speak correctly."

I snapped my dead eyes towards the girls, not knowing which one had said that.

"I've done more in my life than you'll ever know. A drug addict accomplished that, you fucking bitch," I spewed out. In my scrambled mind, I thought about how easy it would be to grab her and watch her lifeless body on the floor.

"I don't know why Nicole ever dated you, you hateful asshole. I'm glad she dumped your ass," said the girl on the left. I remembered I'd briefly seen these girls at prom with Nicole. They were her friends. I laughed hysterically, then went silent.

"Do you want me to show you why Nicole dumped me?"

I tried to get up but fell against the gate. The girls started to laugh at me.

The girl on the right chimed in. "Nicole told me everything about you. You're a fucking crackhead, and everyone knows it. Have fun being homeless."

She spat at me on the ground, and it hit my arm. I grasped the bench with one hand, regaining my composure. "I don't like you, but you're Nicole's friends. Get out of here, both of you. Go home."

The girl on the right flipped her hair. "You don't have to tell us twice, you disgusting crackhead."

I watched as they left and gripped the bench, still the whole time, until I lost my grip and fell to the ground. It was almost dusk, and the stars were coming out. All the memories were flooding back. I could hear the sound of bone colliding with my knife, and I started to scream for it to stop. I saw Paul on top of Lily over and over a thousand times, and the shots I'd fired. I saw her body lying there when I pushed him off. They replayed in front of my eyes over and over. Kill me. I begged God to kill me. "Kill me, please God," I begged the stars. All I got in response were the two stars I'd seen here before. The bigger one had become the same size as the other. They were both the same size and glowed the same. The same dead stars, the same dead humans.

Be Yourself

When I awoke, I let the memories of everything that had happened fill my brain and watched my broken eyes stare into nothingness. The sun beamed down on me as I lay on the bench, making my skin glow. For once, I got up to sit there and stare at the field. I remembered playing here as a boy and could see myself at the batter's box. I stared at it. As I stared at younger me there, I wanted to jump out of my broken body and into my memories. I wanted to be whole again. I wanted Lily to be alive. I wanted to be a good person.

Stumbling to gain my composure, I walked out of the dugout and across the field. Memories surrounded me as I heard a baseball being hit and people cheering. I heard my parents talking to me and telling me I'd done well. I could see Lily standing next to my parents, smiling at me.

As I walked throughout the town in a daze, I found myself wandering down to the south side in hopes of finding anyone or anything. All I could think about was the end for me. There was no way out. This would be it. I just couldn't fucking believe my luck. Everything that could go wrong had. I was about to kick a nearby trash can when I heard someone call out to me.

I saw Trey. He came closer and looked me up and down. I asked what he wanted in a tone of hatred.

"Michael, you don't get this high on your own supply."

I tried to throw a punch at him that Trey easily stepped away from. "What do you know about me? You stopped letting me sell to you. Fuck you, old man."

Trey shook his head. "I don't even recognize that kid that came to the water tower anymore. Look at you."

"Of course I'm not the same person, you moron. If you've been through half of what I've been through, you'd be on your knees crying for God to strike you down."

My words obviously affected him. I still had my language.

Trey looked at me darkly. "I should have never sold to you. I regret ever selling to kids. Maybe God might indeed strike me down, Michael. Or maybe you will. Aren't you named after the archangel?"

I spit at him. "Fuck you, Trey. Everyone I love is dead because of you someway. And James bringing up my father. I'll kill you both."

Trey dusted off his pants and took one good look at me. "Good luck, kid."

I yelled at him to come back and fight me. Fucking coward. He would get what was coming to him.

As I walked, I held my hand out as if to grasp it and hold onto the memory forever. All the sun did was make me look sick and tired. I felt like dying and decided to go to the convenience store nearby to get some water. Not knowing the last time I'd drank water or eaten made me realize I was close to death's door. The abuse of drugs I'd put my body through was starting to show mentally, as I could barely differentiate what was real and what wasn't.

I didn't understand why I hadn't been caught yet, and I didn't understand why I was still alive. Was there any meaning left in my life?

Walking towards the store, I heard a familiar voice call out. I was halfway there and didn't want to turn around because of what I dreaded. The person of that voice made the choice for me as they jogged out in front of me. With dead eyes, I stared at none other than Thomas's friend Connor.

"I came into town a couple of weeks ago when I heard you got arrested. I've been watching you in a way, before I turn you in. Or let you overdose, whichever comes first," he said with a laugh.

Connor looked the same as I remembered him, while I looked like a sickly dog that needed to be put down. I had nothing to say to him and wanted to be on my way. I moved to go around him, but he stood in front of me again.

"Last time we met, I could have killed you. For some time, I was planning on coming back to town to do just that, but you've done it for me."

Connor told me this as he lifted my face with his hands. I swung whatever power I had left in my right hand at his face, which he took on the chin.

"You still hit hard for a dead man. I'll give you that," Connor told me as he walked around in front of me.

"Get the fuck out of here, Michael. You're not even worth the call to the cops."

I mumbled something along the lines of "okay" and made my way to the gas station.

The chances of Connor being here were so low that I realized it was probably a hallucination. I tried to feel for pain but couldn't due to the drugs. Real or not, he wasn't wrong. I was pathetic, and everything around me had died. I didn't care anymore. There was nothing out there for me in this world.

Finally reaching the gas station and grabbing the door handle, I walked inside looking like a dead man and grabbed a water with some chips. At the counter, I saw a journal and pen for two dollars which I also grabbed. I scrounged up a five and left before the cashier could see my face, as I knew five dollars would cover that. Walking out of there, I had no clue where I'd go. I was nothing but an empty, hollow being filled with memories and regrets. I looked around the neighborhood I was walking down and saw two black birds chase each other, and wished again I could be a bird and fly away. I was stuck to the ground in my broken state.

After walking a considerable distance, I sat down in front of someone's gate, which had a granite porch to the left of it. I opened my chips and drank my water, just staring at the ground. The road looked as cracked and broken as I was. It would never be fixed, just like me. I tried to cry. I wanted Lily to be here to apologize to, but nothing came. I sat there for hours, and not a single car came by, yet I remained awake, filled with agony and pain, just staring into the distance.

"Where did it all go wrong?" I asked myself aloud. Using my sweater, I wiped my tears and stared at the sun setting. I watched as it went lower and lower until darkness surrounded everything.

I figured I needed to write something down, my thoughts all scrambled. I opened the journal I had bought. No one on the planet was worth caring about anymore, but I felt like I needed to try to explain myself.

I used to write about wanting to be free. How I was envious and jealous of birds. Now I realize all of living is pain. The bird flies and is killed by a human, or another creature. The same as me.

My life has been one failure after another. My drug addiction has led—no, fuck it—the people around me all failed me. One by one. I'm sick of playing games in this world. The only freedom for me is death. Maybe that's why my dad or mother did it. Maybe they knew something I didn't.

I know that when I overdose, no one will be coming to save me. My mom won't walk in and say, my poor, poor son. No one is coming to save me. That's been my whole fucking life. I always had to do everything. I feel like I've lived my entire life at the age of seventeen.

Why is everyone around me so incompetent? I needed one person. One person and I probably won't be dead of an overdose. But I couldn't get that.

I lived my way and I have no regrets. I liked it. Death isn't judgmental.

— Michael Ren

I decided I'd made up my mind on what to do. One more walk over to where I could find what I was looking for. One more look for myself and the end of my pain. I got up, took more pills, and finished my water. I looked at the houses around me that reminded me so much of the one I'd grown up in and decided to part ways.

Making my last trip, I walked around town to the graveyard, hoping to find who I was looking for. The dark had consumed all light and made it hard to find anything. After my father died, I'd visited this place many times, which made it easier to navigate even without light.

When I reached the gravestone, I stared at it with no emotion.

Christopher Ren

Loving father and husband

Gone too soon

I looked to my left and right to see if my mother had been buried here, but was met with empty grass. She had no one except me to pay for a funeral, and I'd been absent. She would never be able to rest with her lover. At this point, I'd made up my mind and walked to another gravestone.

Reaching this one didn't provoke any emotions, but I could feel the failure inside me for what I'd done.

Edmund Weber

Loving father and husband

Survived by his wife and child

It was almost identical to my father's, which Lily and I had always remarked on. Maybe my mother and Katrina had decided to do it that way since they'd been so close. This time, looking to my left and right, I found what I was looking for. Fresh roses had been laid on the grave, and I could barely make out what it said through my tears as I read it.

Lily Weber

In loving memory of a daughter filled with grace and fire.

Taken too soon, and to be remembered forever.

I sat next to it in tears. "I'm sorry, Lily. For all of it. Every little piece of it."

My grave would be next to my father's, just like hers was next to hers. I brought my backpack close and drank my water slowly. I sat there and pictured my last visions on earth. Everything that had happened in the previous year.

Everything that had led up to this moment. I looked around and brought my hand out as if to grasp onto the last bit of reality I had. My eyes felt heavy, and I could barely see anymore. In this graveyard of death, I'd decided it would be my final resting place. People go through life, and in some moments, they experience something magical. There are decades where nothing happens, and weeks where decades happen.

I felt as if I'd lived my life to its limit. Everything was used and exhausted, and there was no good end in sight. Clutching my backpack, I saw a light turn on in the graveyard, which I assumed was the groundskeeper making sure no one trespassed. He must have seen me, as I saw him walk out and look in my direction. Soon, he'd be calling the cops, and my life would cease to exist.

Taking the items out of my backpack, I injected a lethal dose of heroin into my arm. While almost passing out, I filled it back up and did another full dose. My vision was blurring to the max, and I grasped for pills and threw them into my mouth, not knowing what they were. All that mattered was that it would be enough to relieve me of the chronic pain I had caused myself.

I felt myself start to sputter and my heart rate fluctuate as I fell on my back and looked at the night sky. Lily would have loved tonight's sky. I turned toward her gravestone, my vision now almost completely gone. I started to see fluorescent lights, red and blue, as I stared at the stars. The constellations all lit up and seemed to float in front of my eyes. I heard the noises of sirens and felt my body unable to move. As I lay there, my eyes settled on those two stars I'd seen before. They were as beautiful as ever and had combined into one that bathed me in eternal light. I reached my hand towards them as my body shuddered and took my last breath while the night sky was filled with lights, both natural and unnatural.

Epilogue

The waves came up to me and turned back to the ocean right as they were about to hit me. I looked out in front of me and saw the sea I'd loved, only now it was a bright red color with a bright red background. The mountains and rocks all around me were the same, but the sea was red. The rain descended around me, but I felt nothing, and I looked up to see two birds swirling above. They didn't seem to feel the rain either.

I wanted to get up and get a closer look when I realized someone was in my lap. She looked beautiful, with blonde hair that flowed across her body like an angel. I wanted to ask who she was, but I couldn't find the words.

"Did you find what you were looking for?" the girl in my lap asked me.

Overlooking the sea, it came up to me again and went back. I took time to think about my answer. "I was a failure," was what I said while I drew in the sand, which magically fixed itself where I'd indented it. She seemed to shift in my lap, reaching out her arm as the waves came in, and I saw she was able to touch it. The girl let the water trickle through her fingers.

"Did you enjoy it?"

I shook my head in frustration, as I wanted to tell her how much of a failure I was. She got up from my lap and walked towards the water, but I could hear her voice all the same. "You don't have to hate yourself for what you did. Your actions were your own."

I slipped into fading memories. Walking with Lily to the diner. Her making a joke about how I was only going to get a soda. Her walking around town with me smiling at me in the rain. I smiled back at her and tried to talk to her, but it was gone.

Another one appeared. I saw a baseball coming towards me. Strike one, the person behind me yelled. I was holding a bat, and the person in front of me looked ready to throw. "You got this, Michael," I heard my dad say, and I looked towards him. As I looked, I heard strike two, and he was gone.

Suddenly I walked towards where the memory had been and saw Nicole and me talking in the car. I saw her say forever, and I in turn said it back. Forever, I said aloud, but they couldn't hear me.

I yelled back to her as she walked farther into the ocean. "I destroyed everything with my actions. I am the complete definition of a failure."

She reached down to run her fingers through the water as she walked farther away. "You lived your way, and you'll die your way."

I already knew this. Everything I did would be with me until I died. Why was I being reminded? I tried to get up and talk to her, but my body was unable to move at the shoreline.

The farther she walked away, the sadder I got. "Don't leave me," I called out, but she was too far away to hear by then. I was left watching her walk into a red sea that would swallow her whole as I sat there. She looked towards me, and I was finally able to see her before the waves completely swallowed her.

"I'll always love you. Take care, Michael."

I reached my hand out to touch her, and she mirrored me with the same movement. For one moment, I felt a connection of our hands touching, and that was it.

Sitting there, I was utterly alone. Now that she was gone, the water surprisingly came up and touched me. I tried to get up and was allowed to. I ran into the waves to follow her to wherever she'd gone. As I ran, the water kicked around me and felt like nothing, as if I were running in the air. I would run forever to where she was. I got to where I thought she'd disappeared and looked around. I saw her smiling in the same spot I'd just left and started to run back. I would chase her to the ends of eternity, not to be alone. To be human. To have someone with me. To not be in the dark. As I reached her, she looked up at me and stared into my soul. I heard her voice in my head as she stared at me.

"You don't have to run anymore."

Fin

About the Author

Tanner Peterson grew up in California and currently lives in the United States with his wife, Audrey, whose belief in him made this book possible. BURNOUT is his debut novel, written for anyone who has lived through the reality of drug abuse or watched it consume someone they love. He hopes this is the first of many novels to come.